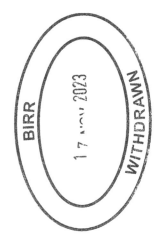

ABOUT THE AUTHOR

JACQUELINE WOODSON is the bestselling author of more than two dozen award-winning books for young adults, middle graders and children, including the *New York Times* bestselling memoir *Brown Girl Dreaming*, which won the 2014 National Book Award, the Coretta Scott King Award, a Newbery Honor Award, an NAACP Image Award, and the Sibert Honor Award. Woodson was recently named the Young People's Poet Laureate by the Poetry Foundation. She lives with her family in Brooklyn, New York.

PRAISE FOR *ANOTHER BROOKLYN*

"Woodson's unsparing story of a girl becoming a woman recalls some of the genre's all-time greats: *A Tree Grows in Brooklyn*, *The Bluest Eye* and especially, with its darkly poetic language, *The House on Mango Street*." —*Time*

"Woodson does for young black girls what short story master Alice Munroe does for poor rural ones: She imbues their everyday lives with significance." —*Elle*

"In Jacqueline Woodson's soaring choral poem of a novel...four young friends...navigate the perils of adolescence, mean streets, and haunted memory in 1970s Brooklyn, all while dreaming of escape." —*Vanity Fair*

"Woodson writes lyrically about what it means to be a girl in America, and what it means to be black in America. Each sentence is taut with potential energy, but the story never bursts into tragic flames; it stays strong and subtle throughout."
—*Huffington Post*

"*Another Brooklyn* joins the tradition of studying female friendships and the families we create when our own isn't enough, like that of Toni Morrison's *Sula*, Tayari Jones' *Silver Sparrow* and *Zami: A New Spelling of My Name* by Audre Lorde. Woodson uses her expertise at portraying the lives of children to explore the power of memory, death and friendship."
—*Los Angeles Times Book Review*

"It is the personal encounters that form the gorgeous center of this intense, moving novel...Structured as short vignettes, each reading more like prose poetry than traditional narrative, the novel unfolds as memory does, in burning flashes, thick with detail."
—*New York Times Book Review*

"With *Another Brooklyn*, Jacqueline Woodson has delivered a love letter to loss, girlhood, and home. It is a lyrical, haunting exploration of family, memory, and other ties that bind us to one another and the world."
—*Boston Globe*

"Woodson manages to remember what cannot be documented, to suggest what cannot be said. *Another Brooklyn* is another name for poetry."

—*Washington Post*

"In this elegant and moving novel, Jacqueline Woodson explores the beauty and burden of growing up *Girl* in 1970s Brooklyn through the lens of one unforgettable narrator. The guarded hopes and whispered fears that August and her girlfriends share left me thinking about the limits and rewards of friendship well after the novel's end. Full of moments of grief, grace, and wonder, *Another Brooklyn* proves that Jacqueline Woodson is a master storyteller."

—Angela Flournoy, author of the
National Book Award finalist *The Turner House*

"*Another Brooklyn* is a sort of fever dream, containing both the hard truths of life and the gentle beauty of memory. The story of a young girl trying to find herself in the midst of so many conflicting influences and desires swallowed me whole. Jacqueline Woodson has such an original vision, such a singular voice. I loved this book."

—Ann Patchett,
New York Times bestselling author of *Commonwealth*
and *This Is the Story of a Happy Marriage*

"And Sister Jacqueline Woodson sings memory. Her words like summer lightning get caught in my throat, and I draw August up from Southern roots to a Brooklyn of a thousand names, where she and her three 'sisters' learn to navigate a new season. A new herstory. Everywhere I turn, my dear Sister Jacqueline, I hear your words, a wild sea pausing in the wind. And I sing."

—Sister Sonia Sanchez

"Jacqueline Woodson's *Another Brooklyn* is another kind of book, another kind of beautiful, a lyrical, hallucinatory, heartbreaking, and powerful novel. Every gorgeous page leads to another revelation, another poignant event or memory. This is an incredible and memorable book."

—Edwidge Danticat, author of *Claire of the Sea Light*

"Jacqueline Woodson's spare, emphatic novel about young women growing up in 1970s Bushwick brings some of our deepest silences—about danger, loss, and black girls' coming-of-age—into powerful lyric speech. *Another Brooklyn* is heartbreaking and restorative, a gorgeous and generous paean to all we must leave behind on the path to becoming ourselves."

—Tracy K. Smith, Pulitzer Prize–winning author of *Life on Mars* and *Ordinary Light*

"Jacqueline Woodson's *Another Brooklyn* is a wonder. With a poet's soul and a poet's eye for image and an ear for lyrical language, Woodson delivers a moving meditation on girlhood, love, loss, hurt, friendship, family, faith, longing, and desire. This novel is a love letter to a place, an era, and a group of young women whom we've never seen depicted quite this way or this tenderly. Woodson has created an unforgettable, entrancing narrator in August. I'll go anywhere she leads me."

—Naomi Jackson,
author of *The Star Side of Bird Hill*

"Grief and friendship are the hallmarks of this story that leaps from the pages in a musical prose that is exacting and breathtaking. Woodson illustrates the damning invisibility and unrelenting objectification of girls in this tender tale that effuses a spirit of unrelenting hopefulness. *Another Brooklyn* is a tableau of the personal and the collective that is at once graceful, restrained, and potent. It is an exquisite telling."

—Lauren Francis-Sharma,
author of *'Til the Well Runs Dry*

ANOTHER BROOKLYN

JACQUELINE WOODSON

ONEWORLD

A Oneworld Book

First published in Great Britain and Australia
by Oneworld Publications, 2017

ISBN 978-1-78607-083-8 (hardback)
ISBN 978-1-78607-084-5 (export paperback)
ISBN 978-1-78607-085-2 (eBook)

Printed and bound in Great Britain by Clays Ltd, St Ives plc

This is a work of fiction. While, as in all fiction, the literary
perceptions and insights are based on experience, all names,
characters, places, and incidents either are products of the author's
imagination or are used fictitiously.

Oneworld Publications
10 Bloomsbury Street
London WC1B 3SR
United Kingdom

Stay up to date with the latest books,
special offers, and exclusive content from
Oneworld with our monthly newsletter

Sign up on our website
oneworld-publications.com

For Bushwick (1970–1990)
In Memory

Keep straight down this block,
Then turn right where you will find
A peach tree blooming.

—RICHARD WRIGHT

ANOTHER
BROOKLYN

1

For a long time, my mother wasn't dead yet. Mine could have been a more tragic story. My father could have given in to the bottle or the needle or a woman and left my brother and me to care for ourselves—or worse, in the care of New York City Children's Services, where, my father said, there was seldom a happy ending. But this didn't happen. I know now that what is tragic isn't the moment. It is the memory.

=

If we had had jazz, would we have survived differently? If we had known our story was a blues with a refrain running through it, would we have lifted our heads, said to each other, *This is memory* again and again until the living made sense? Where would we be now if we had known there was a melody to our madness? Because even though Sylvia, Angela, Gigi, and I came together like a jazz improv—half notes tentatively moving toward one another until the ensemble found its footing and the music felt like it had always been playing—we didn't have jazz to know this was who we were. We had the Top 40 music of the 1970s trying to tell our story. It never quite figured us out.

=

The summer I turned fifteen, my father sent me to a woman he had found through his fellow Nation of Islam brothers. An educated sister, he said, who I could talk to. By then, I was barely speaking. Where words had once flowed easily, I was suddenly silent, breath snatched from me, replaced by a melancholy my family couldn't understand.

Sister Sonja was a thin woman, her brown face all angles beneath a black hijab. So this is who the therapist became to me—the woman with the hijab, fingers tapered, dark eyes questioning. By then, maybe it was too late.

Who hasn't walked through a life of small tragedies? Sister Sonja often asked me, as though to understand the depth and breadth of human suffering would be enough to pull me outside of my own.

=

Somehow, my brother and I grew up motherless yet halfway whole. My brother had the faith my father brought him to, and for a long time, I had Sylvia, Angela, and Gigi, the four of us sharing the weight of growing up *Girl* in Brooklyn, as though it was a bag of stones we passed among ourselves saying, *Here. Help me carry this.*

=

Twenty years have passed since my childhood. This morning, we buried my father. My brother and I stood shoulder to shoulder at the gravesite, willows weeping down around us, nearly bare-branched against the snow. The brothers and sisters from mosque surrounding us. In the silver light of the morning, my brother reached for and found my gloved hand.

Afterward, at a diner in Linden, New Jersey, my brother pulled off his black coat. Beneath it, he wore a black turtleneck and black wool pants. The black kufi his wife had knitted for him stopped just above his brow.

The diner smelled of coffee and bread and bleach. A neon sign flickered EAT HERE NOW in bright green, dusty silver tinsel draping below it. I had spent Christmas Day at the hospital, my father moaning for pain medication, the nurses too slow in responding.

A waitress brought my brother more hot water for his mint tea. I picked at my eggs and lukewarm home fries, having eaten the bacon slowly to tease my brother.

You hanging in, Big Sis? he asked, his deep voice breaking up a bit.

I'm good.

Still whole?

Still whole.

Still eating pork and all the other Devil's food, I see.

Everything but the grunt.

We laughed, the joke an old one from the afternoons I had snuck off with my girls to the bodega around the corner for the foods I was forbidden to eat at home and the bits of bacon still on my plate.

You still could come stay with me and Alafia you know. Bedrest isn't contagious.

I'm good at the apartment, I said. *Lots to be done there. All his stuff to go through . . . Alafia doing okay?*

She'll be all right. Doctors talk like if she stands up, the baby's gonna just drop right out of her. It's all good. Baby'll be fine.

I started my way into the world two days before July ended but didn't arrive until August. When my mother, crazed from her long labor, asked what day it was, my father said, *It's August. It's August now. Shhh, Honey Baby,* he whispered. *August is here.*

You scared? I asked my brother, reaching across the table to touch his hand, remembering suddenly a photo we had back in SweetGrove, him a new baby on my lap, me a small girl, smiling proudly into the camera.

A little. But I know with Allah all things are possible.

=

We were quiet. Old white couples surrounded us, sipping coffee and staring off. In the back somewhere, I could hear men speaking Spanish and laughing.

I'm too young to be someone's auntie.

You're gonna be too old to be somebody's mama if you don't get busy. My brother grinned. *No judgment.*

No judgment is a lie.

Just saying it's time to stop studying the dead and hook up with a living brother. I know a guy.

Don't even.

I tried not to think about the return to my father's apartment alone, the deep relief and fear that came with death. There were clothes to be donated, old food to throw out, pictures to pack away. For what? For whom?

In India, the Hindu people burn the dead and spread the ashes on the Ganges. The Caviteño people near Bali bury their dead in tree trunks. Our father had asked to be buried. Beside his lowered casket, a hill of dark and light brown dirt waited. We had not stayed to watch it get shoveled on top of him. It was hard not to think of him suddenly waking against the soft, invisible satin like the hundreds of people who had been buried in deep comas only to wake beneath the earth in terror.

———

You gonna stay in the States for a minute?

8

A minute, I said. I'll be back for the baby though. You know I wouldn't miss that.

As a child, I had not known the word *anthropology* or that there was a thing called Ivy League. I had not known that you could spend your days on planes, moving through the world, studying death, your whole life before this life an unanswered question . . . finally answered. I had seen death in Indonesia and Korea. Death in Mauritania and Mongolia. I had watched the people of Madagascar exhume the muslin-wrapped bones of their ancestors, spray them with perfume, and ask those who had already passed to the next place for their stories, prayers, blessings. I had been home a month watching my father die. Death didn't frighten me. Not now. Not anymore. But Brooklyn felt like a stone in my throat.

You should come out to Astoria for a meal soon, a clean meal. Alafia can sit at the table, just not allowed to stand at the stove and cook. But I got us. It's all good.

A minute passed. *I miss him,* he said. *I miss you.*

In my father's long, bitter last days of liver cancer, we had taken turns at his bedside, my brother coming into the hospital room so I could leave, then me waking him so he could go home for a quick shower and prayer before work.

Now my brother looked as though he was seven again, not thirty-one, his thick brow dipping down, his skin too clear and smooth for a man.

I wanted to comfort him. *It's good that he . . .* but the words wouldn't come.

Allah is good, my brother said. *All praise to Allah for calling him home.*

All praise to Allah, I said.

=

My brother drove me to the subway, kissed my forehead, and hugged me hard. When had he become a man? For so long, he had been my little brother, sweet and solemn, his eyes open wide to the world. Now, behind small wire-rimmed glasses, he looked like a figure out of history. Malcolm maybe. Or Stokely.

I'll be by day after tomorrow to help you out, cool?

I'm good!

What—you got a man over there you don't want me to meet?

I laughed.

Still doing the Devil, I bet.

I slapped at him and got out of the car. *Love you.*

Love you, too, August.

On the subway heading back to the old apartment, I looked up, startled to see Sylvia sitting across the aisle reading the *New York Times*. She had aged beautifully in the twenty years since I'd last seen her. Her reddish brown hair was cut short now, curly and streaked with gray. Her skin, still eerily bronze against those light eyes, was now etched through with fine wrinkles. Maybe she felt me watching her because she glanced up suddenly, recognized me, and smiled. For several slow seconds, the years fell away and she was Sylvia again, nearly fifteen in her St. Thomas Aquinas school uniform—green and blue plaid skirt, white blouse, and plaid cross bow tie, her belly just beginning to round. As my body seized up with silence again, I remembered Sister Sonja, her hijabbed head bent over her notebook, her fingers going still the first time I cried in her office.

Sylvia.

Oh my God! August! she said. *When did you get back to Brooklyn?*

The child would be a young woman now. I remember hearing she had Sylvia's reddish hair, and that as a newborn, her eyes had been gray.

Somehow I knew the train was pulling into Atlantic Avenue. But the station and everything around me felt far away. Somehow, I rose from my seat. Voice gone again. Body turning to ash.

Maybe Sylvia thought I was coming toward her, ready to hug away the years and forget. Maybe she had already forgotten, the way years allow us to.

You look good, girl, she said.

The train doors opened. It wasn't yet my stop.

But I got off anyway.

13

=

Years erase us. Sylvia sinking back into the dust of the world before I knew her, her baby gone, then her belly, then breasts, and finally only the deep gap in my life where she had once been.

Angela fading next, across the years, just a faint voice on the answering machine when I was home on college break. *I only just heard about Gigi. So awful. Were you there?* Promises to reconnect when both of us were next in New York. Promises she'd find me again. So much air around the lies distance allowed us to tell as she sank back into the world she had become a part of, a world of dancers and actors—redrawn into royalty without a past.

Gigi.

Each week, Sister Sonja said, *Start at the beginning,* her dark fingers bending around a small black notebook, pen poised. Many moments passed be-

14

fore I opened my mouth to speak. Each week, I began with the words *I was waiting for my mother . . .*

The office was small, ivy cascading down from a tiny pot on an otherwise stark windowsill. Maybe it was the ivy that kept me coming back. Every week, I spent forty minutes, my eyes moving from the ivy to Sister Sonja's hijab to her fingers closed around the notebook and pen. Maybe I spoke only because each week I was allowed to look into the brown, angled face of a woman and believe again that my mother was coming soon.

I know when I get there, my brother and I used to sing. *The first thing I'll see is the sun shining golden. Shining right down on me . . .*

How did I get there, to that moment of being asked to start at the beginning? Who had I become?

She's coming, I'd say. *Tomorrow and tomorrow and tomorrow.*

What about your friends? Sister Sonja asked. *Where are they now?*

We're waiting for Gigi, I'd say. *Everyone's waiting for Gigi.*

Sylvia, Angela, Gigi, August. We were four girls together, amazingly beautiful and terrifyingly alone.

This is memory.

=

In eastern Indonesia, families keep their dead in special rooms in their homes. Their dead not truly dead until the family has saved enough money to pay for the funeral. Until then, the dead remain with them, dressed and cared for each morning, taken on trips with the family, hugged daily, loved deeply.

2

The year my mother started hearing voices from her dead brother Clyde, my father moved my own brother and me from our SweetGrove land in Tennessee to Brooklyn. It was the summer of 1973 and I was eight years old, my younger brother four, his thumb newly moving to his mouth in the hot city, his eyes wide and frightened.

The small apartment was on the top floor of a three-story building. My brother and I had never been this high up, and we spent hours staring past the painted-shut windows down to the street below. The people passing beneath us were all beautiful in some way—beautifully thin, beautifully obese, beautifully Afroed, or cornrowed, or bald. Beautifully dressed in bright African dashikis and bellbottomed jeans, miniskirts and halters.

The green of Tennessee faded quickly into the foreign world of Brooklyn, heat rising from cement. I thought of my mother often, lifting my hand to stroke my own cheek, imagining her beside me, explaining this newness, the fast pace of it, the impenetrable gray of it. When my brother cried, I shushed him, telling him not to worry. *She's coming soon,* I said, trying to echo her. *She's coming tomorrow.* And tomorrow and tomorrow and tomorrow.

=

It was during this summer that I first saw Sylvia, Gigi, and Angela. The three of them walked down our block, dressed in halter tops and shorts, arms linked together, heads thrown back, laughing. I watched until they disappeared, wondering who they were, how they . . . *became.*

My mother had not believed in friendships among women. She said women weren't to be trusted. *Keep your arm out,* she said. *And keep women a whole other hand away from the farthest tips of your fingernails.* She told me to keep my nails long.

But as I watched Sylvia, Angela, and Gigi walk past our window, I was struck with something deeply unfamiliar—a longing to be a part of who they were, to link my own arm with theirs and remain that way. Forever.

Another week passed and they appeared again, this time stopping below our window, untwining and doubling a long line of telephone cable, Gigi and Angela turning as Sylvia stood just outside the double ropes, rocking back and forth on the balls of her feet before jumping in. I watched them, my mouth slightly open, intrigued by the effortless flow of them, how each one moved so that the other could continue moving.

My father, brother, and I were different from this. I went through my days connected to them, but inside myself, holding my brother, laughing with my father, always deeply aware of their presence. But it was a presence in shadow, a presence etched in DNA. When I watched my brother and father bending toward each other to speak, I'd see their fluid connection, a *something* I was on the outside of. Maybe this was how my mother and I bent into each other. When she returned, we'd bend this way again. In the meantime, I pressed my face against the hot glass, palms flat against the window, wanting to be on the inside of Sylvia, Angela, and Gigi's continuum.

In late July, my father took a knife to the top window frame, wedging it along the lines of thick green paint until the frame gave in and the sound of the city finally wafted up toward us.

A tinny radio from somewhere on the block seemed to play "Rock the Boat" all day long, and sometimes my brother sang the lyrics around his thumb. *So I'd like to know where, you got the notion. Said I'd like to know where . . .*

From that window, from July until end of summer, we saw Brooklyn turn a heartrending pink at the beginning of each day and sink into a stunning gray-blue at dusk. In the late morning, we saw the moving vans pull up. White people we didn't know filled the trucks with their belongings, and in the evenings, we watched them take long looks at the buildings they were leaving, then climb into station wagons and drive away. A pale woman with dark hair covered her face with her hands as she climbed into the passenger side, her shoulders trembling.

My brother and I were often alone. My father's job in the Men's Section at Abraham & Straus Department Store was downtown, and he left just after sunrise to take the B52 bus. We had never been on that bus or any city bus. Buses were as foreign to us as the black and brown boys on the street below, shooting bottle caps across chalk-drawn numbers, their hands and knees a dusty white at the end of the day. Sometimes the boys looked up at our window. More than once, a beautiful one winked at me. For many years, I didn't know his name.

Early one morning, as my brother and I took our place by the window, cereal bowls in our laps, a young boy pulled a wrench from his pocket, used it to remove the cap from the fire hydrant below us, then turned the top of the hydrant until white water pounded into the street. We watched the water for hours. Children we didn't know but suddenly hated with a jealousy thick enough to taste ran through it, their undershirts and cutoffs sticking to their brown bodies. I saw Sylvia, Angela, and Gigi again that day, pulling each other into the water, their voices floating up to our window.

Is she laughing at us? my brother asked. *That red-haired girl. She just looked up at our window and laughed.*

Shush, I said. *She isn't even anybody.*

I was beginning to hate them. I was beginning to love them.

Sometimes, Angela stood apart from the others, biting fiercely at her nails, her short Afro dripping. The high yellow of her skin was as familiar as Tennessee to me. At the small church our mother took us to sometimes, four sisters who looked like Angela sat up front, their hair straightened, braided, and white-ribboned, their backs straight. As their father preached, I watched them, wondering what it was like to walk the edge of holy. *For God so loved the world,* their father would say, *he gave his only begotten son.* But what about his daughters, I wondered. What did God do with his daughters?

=

My father had grown up in Brooklyn but joined the military at eighteen and was stationed at a base near Clarksville, Tennessee. Then Vietnam. Then my mother and SweetGrove. He was missing a finger on each hand, the pinky on his left, and on his right hand, the thumb. When we asked him how it happened, he wouldn't answer, so my brother and I spent hours imagining ways to lose two fingers in a war—knives, bombs, tigers, sugar-diabetes, the list went on and on. His parents had grown old and died only a block from where we now lived. That summer, when we begged him to let us go outside during the day, he shook his head. *The world's not as safe as you all like to believe it is,* he said. *Look at Biafra,* he said. *Look at Vietnam.*

I thought of Gigi, Sylvia, and Angela walking arm in arm through the streets below our window.

How safe and strong they looked. How impenetrable.

One Sunday morning, on the way to the small church my father had found for us, a man wearing a black suit stopped him. *I've been sent by the prophet Elijah, in the name of Allah*, he said, *with a message for you, my beautiful black brother.*

The man looked at me, his eyes moving slowly over my bare legs. *You're a black queen*, he said. *Your body is a temple. It should be covered.* I held tighter to my father's hand. In the short summer dress, my legs seemed too long and too bare. An unlocked temple. A temple exposed.

The man handed my father a newspaper and said, *As-Salaam Alaikum*. Then he was gone.

In church behind the preacher, there was a picture of our Lord Jesus Christ, white and holy, his robe pulled open to show his exposed and bleeding heart.

The Psalm tells us, the preacher said, *I call on the Lord in my distress and he answers me.*

Gold light poured in through a small stained glass window. My father lifted his gaze, saw what I saw—the way the light danced across the folding chairs, the rows of laps, the buckling hardwood floor. Then the sun shifted, melting the light back into shadow. What was the *message for you, my beautiful black brother*, in all that church light? What was it for any of us?

Behind me, an old woman moaned an Amen.

——

The streetlights had come on and from our place at the window, my brother and I could see children running back and forth along the sidewalk. We heard them laughing and shouting *Not it! Not it! Not it!* We could hear the Mister Softee ice cream truck song weaving through it all. My brother begged again and again for the world beyond our window. He wanted to see farther, past the small, newly planted tree, past the fire hydrant, past the reflection of our own selves in the darkening pane.

If anyone had looked up just that minute before, they would have seen the two of us there, as always, watching the world from behind glass. I was ten and my brother was six. Our mother was still in SweetGrove. Our words had become a song we seemed to sing over and over again. *When I grow up. When we go home. When we go outside. When we. When we. When we.* Then my brother's palms were against the window, pushing it out instead of up, shattering it, a deep white gash suddenly pulsing to bright red along his forearm.

How did my father suddenly appear, a thick towel in his hands? Had he been just a room away? Downstairs? Beside us? This is memory. My father's mouth moving but no sound, just my brother's blood pooling on the sill, dripping down onto the jagged glass glinting at our feet. The red lights of an ambulance but no sound. My father lifting my paling brother into his arms but no sound. The trail of silent blood. The silent siren. The silent crowd gathering to watch the three of us climbing into the van.

＝

In the bright white of the hospital room, sound returned, bringing with it taste and smell and touch. The room was too cold. We had not yet eaten dinner. Where was my little brother? A nurse handed me a paper cup of red juice and a Styrofoam plate filled with Nilla wafers. I wanted water. Milk. Meat. There was blood dried to a burnt brown on my T-shirt. Blood on my cutoff shorts. Blood on my light blue Keds. I pressed the cookies together in pairs, chewed slowly.

My mother said Clyde hadn't died in Vietnam. They had the wrong man. *So many brown and black men, who could know?* my mother said. *It could have been anybody. He told me.*

Another nurse wanted to know if I was all right.

Your brother will be fine, she said. *Everything's going to be all right, Sweetie.*

Clyde is fine, my mother said. *He'll be home soon.*

Kings County Hospital. No rooms, just wards. Slide a curtain back and there's a baby crying. Slide another one and there's the girl with the crazily hanging arm. Curtains and children. Nurses and noise. Where was my brother?

You enjoying those cookies, Sugar, the nurse asked.
You was hungry, wasn't you?

The Benguet of the Northern Philippines blind-
fold their dead then sit them on a chair just outside the entrance to their home, their hands and
feet bound.

My mother turned the telegram around and
around in her hands, smiling. Her eyes on the door.

=

For a long time after the broken glass, there was no
room in my head for the newness of Sylvia, Angela,
and Gigi. When they hollered at each other under
my window, I didn't look down. I lay in my bed,
my eyes on the ceiling. A medallion circled the
bulb. Off-white flowers orbited the light, stem to
blossom to stem again. If my mother was coming,
she would be coming now, so close to splintering
glass, my brother's slit-open then sewn-up arm.

When my brother called, *Those girls are out there again*, I didn't answer, curled my toes inside my socks, and turned my face to the wall. Beneath the bandages, black stitches folded my brother's skin back onto itself. I wanted my mother.

3

Soon after the window shattered, my father began to let us go. The front gate first—*Stay inside it. Keep it closed.* Then to the tree in the middle of the block. Then to the STOP sign on the corner. Around the corner to Poncho's bodega, but only together. *Hold your brother's hand.* Then onto the curb, into the street, the handball court, down Knickerbocker, across to the park, the baby swings, the big swings, until my brother and I were finally free.

Some days, I roamed the streets alone, searching for my mother. Would her hair be gray now? Still in an

Afro? Would she be skinnier than I remembered
her or had the years added a weight to her like the
old Italian and Irish women who had moved away,
who had once walked our streets slowly, heavy-
breasted and waist-less. Did she still call Clyde's
name in the night, curse my father, walk through
the land that used to belong to her, walk down to
the water and believe it belonged to her still?

Come with me, I said to my brother again and again.
Let's go look for her.

Before Sylvia, Gigi, and Angela were mine, they arrived at our public school each morning, far away
from me. They called to each other across the yard.
They linked arms and laughed. They curled into
each other to whisper when the teacher's back was
turned. Before I knew their names, I knew the tiny
bones at the back of their necks, the tender curve
of their hairlines. I knew each Peter Pan–collared
shirt and turtleneck they owned. I knew Angela's

scowl as she waited in line in the lunchroom. I knew Sylvia's bronze arm draped around Angela's waist in the school yard. I knew Gigi's voice, a waxed-on Spanish or British or German accent as we pledged in the auditorium.

Every teacher who entered the school yard loved them best, the rest of us sinking into invisibility.

Before they were mine, I stared at their necks, watched their perfect hands close around jump ropes and handballs, saw their brightly polished nails. As they grabbed each other's arms and bounce-walked down the hall, I was sure no ghost mothers existed in their pasts. I truly believed they were standing steadily in the world. I watched them, wanting to have what they had—six feet planted. Right here. Right now.

That year, before we all grew to one height, Sylvia was the tallest. The day we finally became friends,

Angela wore a too-small coat, her thin pale arms protruding from the sleeves. My own jacket was also too small, so I met her eyes first, hoping she'd see we came from the same place—a place where we cornrowed our hair and were unprepared for how quickly winter settled over this city.

The sadness and strangeness I felt was deeper than any feeling I'd ever known. I was eleven, the idea of two identical digits in my age still new and spectacular and heartbreaking. The girls must have felt this. They must have known. Where had ten, nine, eight, and seven gone? And now the four of us were standing together for the first time. It must have felt like a beginning, an anchoring.

I held my nearly flat book bag with both hands.

Why do you stare at us like that, Sylvia said. *What are you looking for?*

Years later I'd remember how shaky her voice was, how I wondered if it was the cold or fear that made it quiver. And in it, there was the slight lilt of Martinique, an island as foreign to me as the Bronx.

Sylvia came closer to me. *Really, I'm asking what are you seeing? When you look at us? I'm not trying to be mean.*

Everything, I said. *I see everything.*

—

You're the one without a mother, aren't you? Sylvia touched my cheek, her mouth so close I could smell her wild cherry Life Saver.

No. That's not me.

It was years before the woman with the hijab. Years before the silence and afternoons of watching ivy cascade down from a windowsill, a pen stilled in a thin dark hand.

The sky was overcast. The school bell was ringing. All around us, children were running toward the entrance. Sylvia took my hand. *You belong to us now*, she said.

And for so many years, it was true.

What did you see in me? I'd ask years later. *Who did you see standing there?*

You looked lost, Gigi whispered. *Lost and beautiful.*

And hungry, Angela added. *You looked so hungry.*

And as we stood half circle in the bright school yard, we saw the lost and beautiful and hungry in each of us. We saw home.

—

Months later, I would learn that Sylvia had arrived the year before me, with her parents and three older sisters from the small island of Martinique. She had spent the summer walking the few blocks her parents allowed with Angela and Gigi, quickly forgetting the French she had always spoken. Her father, who had her same reddish brown hair, thick coils of it, read Hegel and Marcel, quoting them back to Sylvia in a French patois she swore she no longer understood. When she laughed, her beauty stilled me.

Gigi had also come to Brooklyn the year before me, from South Carolina, because her mother's dream was to celebrate her twenty-first birthday in New York City. *Don't do the math*, Gigi said every time someone asked if her mother was her sister. *It just adds up to teen pregnancy.* It was late autumn and we were friends by then, Gigi tucking a heavy braid behind an ear, rolling her eyes.

This would never happen to us, we thought. We knew this could never be *us*.

Some days, Angela's eyes were narrow and distant. When we asked what was wrong, she said, *Nothing! God, why y'all hounding me like I'm a dog!* Those days, we left her to the anger, walking quietly beside her, side-eyeing her hands until they uncurled, reached for ours. *I've always been here*, she said when we asked if there had been anywhere for her before Brooklyn. *I don't have any history*, she said. *Just you guys. Just right here, right now.*

4

We left Tennessee in the night, my father gently shaking my brother and me from sleep. For weeks before, my father and mother had argued. My mother swore she'd bring the butcher knife to bed and sleep with it under her pillow. *Clyde told me about you being with that woman last night,* my mother said. My uncle Clyde had been dead for almost two years by then.

Don't trust women, my mother said to me. *Even the ugly ones will take what you thought was yours.*

=

On Saturdays, my father took us to Coney Island, the three of us riding the double L train to the F train to the last stop. My brother and I watched from the first car window as the Wonder Wheel came into view, then the long-closed Parachute ride, then the Cyclone, and finally, the ocean. We were terrified of the people who hung around the edges of the amusement park—skinny white men covered to their neck in tattoos, stringy-haired women half naked and fighting against heroin-induced nods on the boardwalk, hawkers yanking passersby toward them, promising them thrills, enormous brown women spilling out of tiny bikinis, Puerto Rican children covered in a thick layer of baby oil. We held tight to our father's hands as we walked, begging for the corn dripping with butter and clouds of cotton candy being sold. But there was usually only enough money for a few rides and maybe a hot dog and soda for lunch.

We didn't understand the kind of poverty we lived in. Our apartment was small, furnished by our landlord with a yellow Formica table and chair set in the kitchen, small beds for my brother and me in the single bedroom, and a dark green pullout sofa in the living room. Every evening, after my father kissed us good-night, we heard the squeal of springs as he lifted the sofa into a bed for himself, pillow-less and draped with a thin floral bedspread.

We slept in my father's castaway undershirts in the summer. In the winter, we paired the shirts with dingy long johns, my younger brother's frayed with the hand-me-down scars of my own hard wearing of them.

But my brother and I were never hungry, our faces never ashy, and we were always dressed adequately for whatever the weather brought us. We had seen the truly poor kids, the hard bones of their knees and ankles, the raggedness of their clothes, their eyes hungrily following the Mister Softee ice cream truck as we stood inside the front gate with our father, licking our cones. We were not them. Most days, we had enough.

At night, my father shushed us as we cried. Again, I promised my brother that our mother was on her way.

Why did we leave? he asked.

Because Mommy was talking to Uncle Clyde, I said. *Daddy doesn't believe in ghosts.*

＝

Our mother was sad-eyed and long-limbed like my father, with graceful hands that always seemed to be reaching for something or someone. When Clyde died, those hands slowed, lifted away from her body less often, rarely reached for us.

The first time I watched Angela's pale fingers curl into a fist, I thought of my mother. Light dappled cars, our shoes, the bright gray sidewalk. Angela had been dancing, her leg lifting into an arabesque, her long fingers extending out in front of her. Then just as quickly, she pulled her arms in, her hands closing, her eyebrows twisting with such ferocity, I took a step away from her. *What?* I said. *What is it?* But Angela just shrugged, shoved her hands into her pockets, and shook her head. I wanted to ask, *Where did your hands go, Angela?* I wanted to tell her that when her fingers were still like that, my mother reappeared.

At that moment, a woman had staggered past us slowly, fighting against a nod, her hand swollen and veinless. We watched her, the four of us saying nothing. Her dark skin looked soft enough to touch, a blue sheen beneath the brown.

Where were my mother's still fingers now? I had wondered as I watched the woman, her skin so familiar that I was, for a moment, pulled back in time. Where was my mother's sad-eyed smile? What was the Tennessee air like without me breathing it with her? Lemonade on the porch. The ringing sound of her laughter. The shine and smell of her scalp just after she'd oiled and pressed her hair.

The woman had staggered to the corner, grabbing for the STOP sign and missing it before disappearing around the corner.

How were we to learn our way on this journey without my mother? Even my father on the boardwalk at Coney Island, the music and hawking and rumble of the roller coaster to the right of him, the vast ocean to the left, walked slowly, unsteadily, as though he was as unsure as we were about what step to take next.

==

One evening, my father came home with a small radio. When he turned it on, soft music filled our living room, and my brother and I danced the way we had danced back in Tennessee, lifting our arms, as though our mother was holding our hands, our eyes closed, our heads dipped down.

―

If someone had asked, *Are you lonely?* I would have said, *No*. I would have pointed to my brother and said, *He's here*. I would have lied even as the empty street on rainy afternoons threatened to swallow me whole. If it was the autumn after Sylvia, Angela, Gigi, and I became inseparable, I would have pulled them close, bending deep into the balm of their laughter.

―

A woman named Jennie moved into the apartment below us. She was dark and reedy and wore a long, black wig that stopped at the middle of her back. When she spoke, her voice lilted up. Most of what she said was in Spanish. My father explained a place called the Dominican Republic to us but when she was silent, she could have been from Tennessee. She reminded my brother of our mother. She was beautiful in the same haunted way. *She's almost back now*, my brother said. *She's almost here.* But my father told us to stay away from Jennie.

My father had brought the wooden horsehair brush we used in Tennessee, its bristles still smelling of Dixie Peach and Sulfur 8 hair grease. After washing my brother's hair, I brushed the small kinks out while he bit his lip to keep from crying. *These are Mama's hands*, I whispered. *Close your eyes and it'll be true.* He closed his eyes, reached up, and grabbed my hand with his own. *August*, he said. *I can feel her bones.*

Every two weeks, my father washed my hair then gave me three dollars and sent me wet-headed across the street to Miss Dora's house. Miss Dora was big enough to fill two folding chairs and always sat outside with a mason jar filled with ice and Coca-Cola at her feet. With a towel wrapped around my shoulders, I sat on the ground, the back of my head resting against her enormous thigh, watching the block and wincing through her oiling and cornrowing of my hair. She hummed softly as she braided, and often, I found myself dozing off to "Amazing Grace" or "In the Upper Room."

Miss Dora's son had died in Vietnam. Small American flags adorned her gate and stairs and were hung with a brown extension cord across the bright red aluminum siding that covered the front of her building. A tiny gold flag was pinned above her heart. As the damage of the war staggered, strung-out and bleary-eyed along our block, Miss Dora greeted every ex-soldier who passed. *Glad y'all made it home,* she said. *We'll see my boy in the by and by.*

In the deep heat of summer, we watched as kids circled around the heroin addicts, taking bets on whether or not they'd fall over. Once, a small boy ran down the street, a bent hypodermic needle he'd just found aimed like a gun.

At night, I wrapped my head in fabric torn from an old silk slip of my mother's not remembering how I'd gotten it only that it smelled of her and hair grease now. As my brother and I lay side by side, we listened to the men coming and going from Jennie's apartment—the tinny sound of her bell, the brush of her slippers on the stairs, the men laughing as they made their way up behind her, her quiet *No touch Jennie before you pay Jennie money.*

Money for what? my brother asked into the darkness.

Things. I whispered back. *Just things.*

=

The Tennessee land we called SweetGrove sloped down into a forest of pitch pine, hickory, pecan, and sweet birch trees. Beyond the trees there was more land and where it ended, there was water. The land had belonged to my grandfather on my mother's side. It had come by way of *his* grandfather. Clay dirt and grass waves rolled for acres away from the house my brother and I had been born in. The house itself existed in a state of disrepair—bowed beams, water-stained ceilings, splintering hardwood floors. An ancient wood-burning stove sat beside a newer electric one that no longer worked, a hot plate on the counter between the two. A turquoise refrigerator leaned back against the mustard-colored brick. Water dripped deep inside an upstairs wall, echoing. Sash chain windows were trapped halfway open in the dusty library. Three books held up the third leg of the couch in the living room. On rainy days, the house smelled of decaying wood and briny water. Still, my brother and I moved through the house we'd always known without seeing the ways in which it was sagging into itself. We ran through it laughing, slamming out of and into it, closing our eyes at night then waking in the bright morning inside the pure joy of *Home*.

Clyde was twenty-three. He had graduated from Howard University. He was over six feet tall and had our mother's soft, sweet laugh. In the evenings, long after my brother and I went to bed, our father, mother, and Clyde sat on the sagging front porch and talked about plans for bringing Sweet-Grove back to what it had once been, before any of them were alive to see it so. But neither Clyde nor my father knew how to work that much land. My father was a city boy, and Clyde had, as a boy, loved books and maps and pretty girls, so he never learned the secrets of tasting dirt and spot-spraying webworms and sawflies. The working of the land fell to my mother, whose lovely hands, at the end of the day, were rough, thickened, and red from long hours in the fields.

The year my brother was born, a fire burned the south fields to ash. The following year, a letter from the government revealed that most of the land was now owned by the state of Tennessee due to ignored tax debt and penalties. The house remained ours.

Then Clyde got drafted and went to Vietnam. On the morning we said good-bye, my mother broke down and cried, her pain so raw I covered my ears and shivered. Six months after that, in the winter of 1971, she received a letter.

"We regret to inform you . . ."

This is memory.

Winter and the sound of wind battering the windows. Cold air like a ghost blowing up from the water. My mother slips down heavily onto the floor, brings her knees up to her chin like a little girl, bends her head into them. My father leans against the dead electric stove, palms pressed together in front of his face.

The government owns the pecan trees now. What had once been my family's has been taken. By the government.

5

We came by way of our mothers' memories.

When Gigi was six years old, her mother pulled her in front of the mirror. *It was cracked already,* Gigi said. *I guess that should be a sign. Broken-ass mirror and my crazy mama making promises.*

Those eyes, her mother said, *were your great-grandmother's eyes. She came to South Carolina by way of a Chinaman daddy and mulatto mama.* Gigi stared at her eyes, the slight slant of them, the deep brown. *The hair, too,* her mother said, holding up Gigi's braids. *Heavy and thick like hers.*

The only curse you carry, her mother said, *is the dark skin I passed on to you. You gotta find a way past that skin. You gotta find your way to the outside of it. Stay in the shade. Don't let it go no darker than it already is. Don't drink no coffee either.*

When we had finally become friends, when the four of us trusted each other enough to let the world surrounding us into our words, we whispered secrets, pressed side by side by side or sitting cross-legged in our newly tight circle. We opened our mouths and let the stories that had burned nearly to ash in our bellies finally live outside of us.

It's dark, Gigi said. *But it's got red and blue and gold in it. I look at my arms sometimes and I'm thinking skinny-ass monster arms.* She held her thin arms up into the light, her head lifted, thick braids falling against her back. *And sometimes,* she said, *they look so damn beautiful to me. I don't even know which thing is the truth.*

We circled her, undoing her braids until her hair fell in black coils across her shoulders, then rebraiding and unbraiding them again, telling her how lucky she was to have such thick wavy hair and eyes like a Chinese girl.

When I'm an actress, Gigi said, *I'll be everywhere—TV, movie screen, onstage. Who's that? Who's that?*

When it wasn't wavering around doubt, her voice was deep and sure, and we wanted that, too— *Who's that? Who's that?* we echoed, laughing, our hands on her head, in her hair. *That's that big star, Gigi. Chocolate China Doll!*

What keeps keeping us here? Gigi asked one day, the rain coming down hard, her shirt torn at the shoulder. We didn't know that for weeks and weeks, the lock had been broken on her building's front door. We didn't know about the soldier who slept behind the darkened basement stairwell, how he had waited for her in shadow. We were twelve.

I can't tell anybody but you guys, Gigi said. *My mom will say it was my fault.*

We twisted the long braids up into a crown, used oil and a comb to etch the fine baby hair over her forehead. Dabbed our fingers against our tongues and smoothed out her eyebrows. We wanted to make her broken self know she was still beautiful. *It wasn't you,* we said again and again. *We can kill him,* we said.

We sat on Sylvia's bed counting out what change we had, ran the blocks to Poncho's for a small box of Gillette razor blades, then spent the afternoon practicing how Gigi would hold them when she slashed the soldier. We had heard that Pam Grier slipped them into her hair in *Coffy* and imagined Gigi pulling the blades from her braids just as the soldier stepped out from the darkness.

It'll always be the four of us, right, y'all? Gigi asked.

Of course, we said. *You know that's right,* we said. *Sisters,* we said. We said, *Always.*

But when the soldier finally emerged from behind Gigi's stairs, it was not with a single-edged blade protruding from his neck but with a needle clinched and dripping from his left hand. He had been dead three days when the super found him.

—

Angela's skin was so light you could see blue veins moving through it. She had seen Josephine Baker and Lena Horne and Twyla Tharp on television. Whenever a good song came on, she swayed like water being poured and we watched her, breath caught in our throats, the sadness in her body so deep we had no idea what it was or what it meant or how it got to be there. She was all muscle and sinew. On Saturday afternoons, she showed up on the block with her Joe Wilson's School of Dance bag, her black leotard and tights sweaty and smelly inside it. *My mom was a dancer,* she told us, then quickly grew silent.

Does she still dance, we asked. But Angela turned away from us. Shrugged. Said, *Why you have to be all up in my business?* Said, *Kind of.* Said, *Damn, why's it all have to be so complicated, you know?* She put her face in Gigi's hair and shook until she cried. We said, *We love you, Angela.* We said, *You're so beautiful.* Said, *Just keep dancing. That's all.*

We tried to understand without asking if Mother plus Dance equals Sadness. We waited for her hands to curl into fists. In Sylvia's pink bedroom, we lay down and pressed our ears to her thin chest, listening to the quickening of her heart. *Angela, what is it?* we begged. *Tell us. Please, please tell us. We have blades,* we said. *We can cut somebody.*

We had blades inside our kneesocks and were growing our nails long. We were learning to walk the Brooklyn streets as though we had always belonged to them—our voices loud, our laughter even louder.

But Brooklyn had longer nails and sharper blades. Any strung-out soldier or ashy-kneed, hungry child could have told us this.

＝

I wanted to step inside of Sylvia's skin. Beneath the sweet copper, there lived something diamonded over, brilliant. When we walked, Angela, Gigi, and I vied to be the ones whose arms brushed Sylvia's. When she reached for a hand, ours shot out, lacing our fingers desperately into hers. She was sloe-eyed and wide-mouthed, a beauty that could have just as easily not been so. But hers was all straight teeth and full lips, all

green eyed and new. Long before we were teenagers, her voice was deep, graveled, a woman's voice
on a young girl. Still, it wasn't the skin or the eyes
or the voice I wanted. I simply wanted to *be* Sylvia, to walk through the world as she did, watch
the world through her eyes. *Is that girl laughing
at us*, my brother had asked that first time. And
now I knew Sylvia *was* laughing at us, because
she was laughing at everyone. The same way she
had laughed when her father said *We're going to
America*, his broken English a joke to her, a pup-
pet's mouth moving over newly learned words.
Forever.

What's with America, she asked him. *This America
thing you keep talking and talking about.*

At four, Sylvia was reading books assigned to her
eight-year-old sister. At five, she was made to stay
after school with ten-year-olds, cracking codes in
long division, searching Latin word origins. While
her father quoted French philosophers, Sylvia

stood in front of her dolls, asking her unblinking jury if they could look into the heart of her client and see the innocence there.

My father said study law first, Sylvia told us. *Then everything I love can follow that.*

When we asked, *What do you love?* Sylvia looked around her perfectly pink room and said, *I'm not the boss of me. How the hell would I even know.*

—

Maybe this is how it happened first for everyone— adults promising us their own failed futures. I was bright enough to teach, my father said, even as my dream of stepping into Sylvia's skin included one day being a lawyer. Angela's mom had draped the dream of dancing over her. And Gigi, able to imitate every one of us, could step inside anyone she wanted to be, close her eyes, and be gone. Close her eyes and be *anywhere*.

6

In 1968, the children of Biafra were starving. My brother was not yet born and I was too young to understand what it meant to be a child, to be Biafran, to starve. Biafra was a country that lived only inside my mother's admonitions—*Eat your peas, there are children starving in Biafra*—and in the empty-eyed, brown, big-bellied children moving across my parents' television screen. But long after Biafra melted back into Nigeria, the country from which it had fought so hard to secede, the faces and swollen bellies of those children haunted me. In a pile of old magazines my father kept on our kitchen table in Brooklyn, I found a copy of

Life with two genderless children on the cover and
the words STARVING CHILDREN OF BIAFRA WAR
blared across the ragged white garment of the
taller child.

How do we dream ourselves out of this?

I stared at the cover of *Life*. The children's dis-
trusting eyes stared back at me, too large for their
small, brown heads, too small for their protruding bones and distended bellies. My mother hadn't
lied. There were indeed children suffering. Here
was proof. Here they were on the cover of *Life*
magazine. I spent hours stroking their nearly bald
heads, running my fingers across their almost be-
atific faces. If angels truly existed, I thought, they
had come to earth as Biafran children, haunting
and only halfway here.

No, we were not poor like this. Our bellies were
filled and taut. Our legs were thin but muscled.
Our hair was oiled, clean.

But still.

=

One day a woman wearing a sky-blue skirt suit showed up in front of our building. She had two small children with her, dark brown like Jennie and younger than my brother, who had just turned eight. *My babies,* we heard Jennie yell as she ran down the stairs. *Ay, Dios mío, mis niños han llegado a casa.* When the woman left again, Jennie knocked on our door. *Please watch them,* she whispered. *I go get food.*

The children were tiny and silent, staring up at my brother and me with huge dark eyes. The girl might have been four and the boy not yet two. The girl wore a frilly pink dress, too short and too small. Her shoes were white patent leather. Her feet, sockless. The boy wore a T-shirt and pair of cutoff shorts, a diaper bulging beneath. His white high-top leather baby-shoes had the front cut

67

out to expose his small overhanging toes. I pulled them into our apartment and relocked the door. After a few moments had passed, both started crying. My brother fed them from his bag of potato chips, which they devoured hungrily. We gave them apples and nuts, slices of bologna and Jell-O. Whatever we put in front of them, they ate.

Hours passed. When Jennie finally returned, she was sleepy-eyed, scratching at her arms and legs, her wig at a strange angle. We watched her enter our building, waited for her to come up to our floor. After a long while, we took the children down to her apartment, watched her take them inside absently and close the door. Later, through the floorboards, we could hear them crying.

I went over to our radio, turned the dial until music rose up above every other sound.

7

That year, every song was telling some part of our story. We crowded around the small radio in Sylvia's room and listened. When Gigi's mother wasn't home, we went there after school, waited while Gigi used the key that hung from her neck to unlock the door. There was no couch in the one-room kitchenette, so we sat on the floor around her Close'N Play record player—the volume turned down low. We leaned in to listen as Al Green begged us to lay our heads upon his pillow and Tavares asked us to please remember what they told us to forget. And Minnie Riperton and

Sylvia hit notes so high and long, it felt like the world was ending.

The world *was* ending. We had been girls, wobbling around the apartment in Gigi's mother's white go-go boots and then and then and then.

Little pieces of Brooklyn began to fall away. Revealing *us*.

We envied each other's hair, eyes, butts, noses. We traded clothes and shared sandwiches. Some days we laughed until soda sprayed from our noses and hiccups erupted in our chests.

When boys called our names, we said, *Don't even say my name. Don't even put it in your mouth.* When they said, *You ugly anyway,* we knew they were lying. When they hollered, *Conceited!* we said, *No— convinced!* We watched them dip-walk away, too young to know how to respond. The four of us together weren't something they understood. They understood girls alone, folding their arms across their breasts, praying for invisibility.

═

At eight, nine, ten, eleven, twelve, we knew we were being watched.

So we warned each other about the shoe repair on Gates Avenue, how the old man who reminded us of Geppetto made you wait on the hard wooden seat in the little booth so he could steal glances at your legs and bare feet. *Take somebody with you,* we said. *Don't wear dresses when you go there. He'll offer you a quarter to see your panties.*

When we weren't practicing walking in Gigi's mother's shoes, we were little girls in Mary Janes and lace-up sneakers. When the heels wore down or the soles flapped away from the tops, we were given a dollar and sent to Gates Avenue. *Just a little,* the man said. *Please,* the quarter, held up and gleaming between his thumb and pointer finger as we shook our heads *No* and embarrassed tears we didn't yet understand sprang forward.

The pastor at my church comes up behind me some-times when I'm singing in choir, Gigi said. *I can feel his thing on my back. Don't sing in your church choir. Or if you sing in it, go to another place while you sing.* And she whispered how she was the queen of other places. *Close my eyes and boom, I'm gone. I learned it from my mother,* she told us. *So many days you look in that woman's eyes and she isn't even there!*

But when she is, Gigi said, *she reminds me to go to Hollywood. Tells me I'll be safe there.*

We didn't know to ask *Safe from what? Safe from whom?* We thought we knew.

We promised her she'd be more famous than any-one ever was. We told her no other brown girl had her strange eyes and crazily long hair. We believed ourselves when we said *That's what Holly-wood wants,* and *I can't wait to see you on television,* and *You'll be more famous than Diahann Carroll.*

Don't trust the altar boys, Sylvia warned her, *if you're the only altar girl.*

When she opened her mouth to sing Nina Simone's "Just Like Tom Thumb's Blues," our throats throbbed, our teeth locked together. Sylvia lived deep inside of those notes, halfway hidden from all of us. *They got some hungry women there and man, they'll really make a mess out of you. . . .*

You have to be a singer, we said. *You have to!*

After law, Sylvia said.

We tried to hold on. We played double Dutch and jacks. We chased the ice cream truck down the block, waving our change-filled fists. We frog-jumped over tree stumps, pulled each other into gushing fire hydrants, learned to dance the Loose Booty to Sly and the Family Stone, hustled to Van McCoy. We bought T-shirts with our names and zodiac signs in iron-on letters.

But still, as we slipped deeper into twelve our breasts and butts grew. Our legs got long. Something about the curve of our lips and the sway of our heads suggested more to strangers than we understood. And then we were heading toward thirteen, walking our neighborhood as if we owned it. *Don't even look at us*, we said to the boys, our palms up in front of our faces. *Look away look away look away!*

We pretended to believe we could unlock arms and walk the streets alone. But we knew we were lying. There were men inside darkened hallways, around street corners, behind draped windows, waiting to grab us, feel us, unzip their pants to offer us a glimpse.

We had long lost our razor blades and none of us had ever truly stopped chewing on our nails. But still . . .

I and I and I and I, we chanted. *We and we and we and we.*

We hand-songed *Down down baby, down by the roller coaster. Sweet, sweet baby I'ma never let you go* because we wanted to believe we were years and years away from sweet, sweet babies. We wanted to believe we would always be connected this way. Sylvia, Gigi, and Angela had moved far past my longest fingernail, all the way up my arm. Years had passed since I'd heard my mother's voice. When she showed up again, I'd introduce my friends to her. I'd say, *You were wrong, Mama. Look at us hugging. Look at us laughing. Look how we begin and end each other.*

I'd say, *Can you see this, Mama? Can you?*

A man who used to be a boy on our block walked the streets in his army uniform, armless. He'd learned how to hold a syringe between his teeth and use his tongue to shoot the dope into the veins near his armpit.

My brother and I watched him at night from our window, watched his head dipping down like a bird tucking itself beneath its own wing.

Don't ever do dope, my brother said to me.

You either.

I won't, my brother said.

My brother and I woke to the smell of another house burning somewhere too far away to see, and he said he'd be a fireman maybe. Or an astronaut. Or a scientist, a cop, a drummer in a rock band, a farmer.

A farmer. Because once in SweetGrove, there had been a farm.

I watched my brother watch the world, his sharp, too-serious brow furrowing down in both angst and wonder. Everywhere we looked, we saw the people trying to dream themselves out. As though there was someplace other than this place. As though there was another Brooklyn.

August, my brother said again and again. *Look there. And there. And there.*

We still shared the one bedroom in our apartment, our twin beds only feet apart. We searched for each other first thing in the morning. *Hey,* we said. *Hey yourself. Hay is for horses. Love you. Love you, too,* we whispered each night before we closed our eyes. We reached across the space and entwined our fingers, our hands growing sweaty in the dark. We held on.

What's in that jar, Daddy?

You know what's in that jar.

You said it was ashes. But whose?

You know whose.

Clyde's?

We buried Clyde.

Mine?

This is memory.

8

That was the summer the lights went out in New York City and people looted the stores on Broadway then rode through our neighborhood in convertibles, the tops down, holding boxes of shoes and television sets and pawned fur coats over their heads. My brother and I watched them from our window. The streets, my father said again and again, were too dangerous for anyone in their right mind. We lit candles, heated up cans of SpaghettiOs on the stove, the food in our fridge going bad as my father searched the neighborhood stores for bags of ice. If Biafra and Vietnam were more dangerous than my brother and I understood, the Blackout felt like the end of the world. We heard the horns and sirens moving through the night, saw the hawkers holding their stolen boxes into the air, shouting out prices. In the morning, our father let us go as far as the front gate, where we watched an old woman carrying an armful of looted dry-cleaned clothes up the block, the plastic glistening, her wide grin nearly toothless. We saw two boys sharing a pair of new roller skates, one still carrying the box beneath his arm. We saw teenagers running toward Broadway and asked again and again if we could go. *It's stealing,* my father said. *We don't steal.*

We had heard for years that the shop owners on Broadway were white and lived in fancy houses in places like Brentwood, Rego Park, Laurelton. We knew that financing meant watching neighbors throw broken couches and torn mattresses into the alley between houses long before they were paid off. So as we watched the looters move through the neighborhood selling TVs and radios and shoes and dry cleaning they'd taken from window-smashed stores, my brother and I felt a

ANOTHER BROOKLYN

longing to be a part of the free stuff spilling out
along Broadway. Still, my father warned us not to
leave the front gate. And meant it.

That was the summer every park and every school
building gave out Free Lunch—brown paper bags
holding plastic-wrapped bologna sandwiches and
sugar-sweetened orange juice in foil-sealed cups.
We watched hungry kids line up in the heat, waiting for food, hoping a neighbor was volunteering
who would sneak them an extra bag. In the hot
refrigerator-less days with my father broke from
the work lost at Abraham & Straus, my brother
and I stood on a line that wrapped around the
park and leaned against the chain-link fence as we
slowly moved forward. I looked for Sylvia, Angela,
and Gigi—afraid I'd see them, hungry and hot like
us. Reaching for the brown bags with ashamed
and ashy hands.

The last of the white people began fading. We
didn't know the German woman's name. She was

snow-haired, small and thick, with adult sons who used to come with their children on Sundays. The children, three boys, would not play with us. In the summer, they sat on their grandmother's stoop in their collared shirts and blond crew cuts watching the brown boys in the street spin wooden tops wrapped with graying string. Their fathers had the same cuts, the same pastel-colored collared shirts. In the late afternoon, when the fathers appeared at the top of the stoop, the boys rose and they all made their way to identical station wagons parked one behind the other at the sidewalk. As the cars pulled away, the boys stared at us. Sometimes, the littlest one waved.

The brown boys who had moved to the sidewalk to let the cars pass ran back to the middle of the street and resumed their game. But with the pastel boys gone now, it was hard not to see the brown boys differently in their cutoffs and dirty white T-shirts, ashy kneed, chipped wooden tops violently spinning.

We didn't know the Italian family or the Irish sisters who dressed alike and left their building each morning, pulling identical shopping carts, returning each evening with A&P bags. We didn't know the man who yelled at the boys in the street in a language none of them understood or the curly redheaded family with the mother who always looked as though she'd just had a good cry.

But we knew their moving vans. We knew their cars. We knew the people who came to help, checked their cars many times, then glared at the boys in the street. We knew the sticks for stickball games weren't weapons. We knew the spikes at the bottom of wooden spinning tops weren't meant to hurt anything but other spinning tops. We knew the songs the boys sang *Ungawa, Black Power. Destroy! White boy!* were just songs, not meant to chase white people out of our neighborhood.

Still, they fled.

They left driving their cars. They left in the back-seats of the cars of sons and daughters. They put FOR SALE signs on their homes but left before the buildings sold. They rented to single mothers and junkies, Puerto Ricans and Blacks, anyone with the deposit, the first month's rent, and the promise of a job somewhere. They put mattresses and broken-legged tables and boxes of old books out on the street.

Their cars and vans and trucks parted the brown boys, signaled right at the corner, and left our neighborhood forever.

=

My brother had discovered math, the wonder of numbers, the infinite doubtless possibility. He sat on his bed most days solving problems no eight-year-old should understand. *Squared,* he said, *is absolute. No one in the world can argue algebra or geometry. No one can say pi is wrong.*

Come with me, I begged.

But my brother looked up from his numbers and said, *She's gone, August. It's absolute.*

=

Late in the autumn, the woman returned for Jennie's children. She carried the little one out in her arms, the older one, skipping ahead, not looking back, the baby screaming.

What the hell is going on? My father asked.

They're taking Jennie's children.

I had oiled and braided the older one's hair. Three cornrows front to back tied with a blue Goody ribbon. I had fed them cereal and pastrami sandwiches, grits and eggs. I had put Vaseline on their arms and legs, used a wet washcloth to wipe milk from around their mouths and sleep from the corners of their eyes. I had read to them and sang to them, dampened toilet tissue to wipe crust from their noses. When the girl smiled, her teeth were stunningly white.

The girl, ribbon gone now, skipped around the corner and disappeared. Long after they were out of sight, my brother swore he could hear the baby crying.

===

I imagined the women my father brought home taking a place until my mother returned. Each *Shhh, my kids are sleeping.* Each *Oh lord, look at your precious babies!* brought her closer. I lay in bed and listened as the clink of ice in glasses and the hushed laughter gave way to sighs and moans. I imagined waking up with a new woman, her hair in curlers, holding her robe closed with one hand, asking if I wanted pancakes or cereal, scouring the cabinets for the last of the Aunt Jemima Syrup, sprinkling a bit of cinnamon and sugar when there was none. I imagined strong, sure hands pulling my hair into tight cornrows, telling my brother to take his thumb out of his mouth, kissing my father on the lips as he headed off to work.

I imagined four of us at the kitchen table, the thick stink of boiling chitterlings gone, replaced by hot sauce and white rice and the woman who came to stay until my mother returned asking if I wanted a little or a lot.

Years later, I would tell this to Sister Sonja, wanting her to know that I had dreamed our family whole again. That I believed wholeness was on its way.

=

In a jar on the counter of Poncho's store there were pickled pig's feet that he'd scoop out into brown paper. When you said, *I want to choose my own,* Poncho said, *No choosing! I choose!* his old-man eyes moving over your body. And if you were hungry enough, you let him.

I imagined the four of us—brother, father, new woman, me—sucking the last of the pickled meat from the pig's-foot bone, wrapping cartilage and bone back into the brown paper, washing it down with Dr Pepper.

Pork rinds were packaged and sold for fifteen cents. With hot sauce sprinkled into the plastic bag, you almost had a meal. My brother ate his without the sauce, sometimes adding more salt.

On good days, our father took us around the corner and let us buy ham-and-cheese heroes, the boiled ham cut into thin slices and layered over Italian bread already spread thick with mayo. Some days my brother preferred the square cuts of spiced ham with its tiny speckles of white fat.

That was before.

The woman who came didn't tiptoe through our room in the night, didn't ask for *just a taste* when my father offered his whiskey, didn't sit with us eating pig's feet and spiced ham. She came by way of the Nation of Islam, her head wrapped, her dark dress draping down below her ankles. She said, *My name is Sister Loretta,* her body a temple, covered and far away from my father's, her thin face free of the swine-filled makeup with which unenlightened women painted their faces. She said *I know how amazing and lovely I am.* When she looked down at us and smiled, her dark face broke into something open and hungry and beautiful.

She said, *Your father is ready to change his life.* She said, *The food you're eating is the white devil's plan to kill our people.*

She came into our apartment on a Sunday morning, pulling down dusty pots and pans from the cabinet to wash in warm, soapy water, humming softly as she worked, my father at the table, reading from the Qur'an, a watery Brooklyn sunlight falling over the pages. Her hands were large and moved as though they'd always known our tiny kitchen with its yellowing sink and peeling linoleum counter. I watched them, imagining they were my mother's hands and that we were again in SweetGrove with our broken stove and dusty bookshelves. I sat in the kitchen doorway, my knees pulled up to my chin, eyes lifted toward her. Her breasts were heavy beneath the dark dress but she wasn't a heavy woman. Still, her body seemed to hold promises of curves, of the soft and deep spaces I was just beginning to understand. One day I'd have full breasts, hips, and large hands. One day, my body would tell the world stories beneath the fabric of my clothes.

===

Sister Loretta made us navy beans and eggplant Parmesan. She said no more collard greens or lima beans and my brother and I said *I can dig that,* because we were learning to speak jive talk. She pulled us to her, looked into our eyes, and said jive talk would keep us uneducated and in the ghetto. We believed her and whispered jive only when she wasn't near. When she rang our bell, I took the stairs two at a time to be the first one to her. She hugged me quickly then pushed me away, saying there was so much work to do. The bags of raw peanuts my father brought home to boil and salt were erased. Our beloved boiled-and-spiced-ham heroes, our potatoes both sweet and white, all gone. *The white devil's poison,* she said. *The white devil's swine. Slave food,* she said. *And we're nobody's slaves anymore.* She came by way of the Honorable Elijah Muhammad, messenger of Allah. She said Allah was God and when we said *God is white 'cause his son is Jesus,* she shook her head, looked around at the layer of dust covering everything in our apartment, and shook her head again. She said, *I think I can handle this if this is what Allah has planned for me.*

She came in the daytime, mop and bucket in hand, and showed me how to pull on yellow rubber gloves. Together we attacked the black dirt collecting between the moldings while I told her stories of SweetGrove, how beautiful my mother looked when she walked through the woods toward the water. *I used to walk with her,* I said, hearing again the sound of pine needles crunching under our feet.

You would like SweetGrove, I said. *So much quieter there.*

All is right with Allah, Sister Loretta said. *With Allah, joy again is possible.*

We kneeled together beside a bucket of Cloroxwater, stiff brushes circling the linoleum until a pale green replaced the brown edges of the kitchen floor. In the late afternoon, we spread our prayer rugs and kneeled again toward Mecca.

Just as Sister Loretta promised, Allah healed us. The caterpillar of a keloid moving from the top of my brother's forearm nearly to his wrist faded to a reddish brown. He was proud of the scar, holding his thin arm up, his hand fisted like Huey Newton's.

It could have been worse, the Nation of Islam brothers told my father. Allah had prevailed. The shards of glass could have landed on others below. A vein could have been hit. My brother could have lost his arm. My father could have chosen that evening to take a long walk around the neighborhood, maybe stop after work for a drink.

We lived inside our backstories. The memory of a nightmare stitched down my brother's arm. My mother with a knife beneath her pillow. A white devil we could not see, already inside our bodies, slowly being digested. And finally, Sister Loretta, dressed like a wingless Flying Nun, swooping down to save us.

=

The children of Biafra faded into news images of children starving in the ghettos of Chicago, Los Angeles, New York. We stared at the TV, watching the news cameras pan over neighborhoods then close in on children who stared back, hungry and questioning. In New York, the cameras found Puerto Rican street gangs laughing and wrestling as a somber man warned us of their danger. At the window, my brother searched the block for cameras.

=

While my brother and I cleaned the wooden cabinet doors and polished the glass knobs, Sister Loretta made us bean pies and scalloped turnips with cheese sauce, beets with orange glaze, curried rice, broiled steaks, and asparagus. She came in the late afternoon with chicken she had bought from the kosher butcher and told us that only the Jews and the people of Allah knew how to eat to live. We called her Sister Mama Loretta when we forgot our true mother was coming soon, and begged her to remove her hijab so we could see her hair. After searching for signs of my father and finding none, she pulled the black fabric back to show us the short natural living beneath it. She cornrowed my hair then wrapped my head and promised me I would grow up to be as beautiful as Lola Falana if I ate the right food, followed the messenger Elijah Muhammad, gave all praise to Allah, and remained modest. So I pressed my legs tight together, draped baggy shirts over my new breasts, and promised her I'd remain the sacred being Allah had created. But I was lying.

In the early mornings, I kneeled toward Mecca and prayed silently for my mother—that she would return to us in the darkness, kissing us out of sleep. I prayed that my own brain, fuzzy with clouded memory, would settle into a clarity that helped me to understand the feeling I got when I pressed my lips against my new boyfriend, Jerome's, his shaking hands searching my body. I knew I was lost inside the world, watching it and trying to understand why too often I felt like I was standing just beyond the frame—of everything.

—

Sister Loretta became my partner in prayer, the two of us together in a room separated from my father and brother. Honorable Elijah was God's chosen messenger. We were Allah's chosen people, clean living now, our heads covered during prayer, our bodies free of the foods that were killing us, our hearts and minds moving toward a deeper understanding.

When night came, she left us.

Still . . .

In Uganda, the Baganda people prepare a grave for each person when they are still children.

9

I refused to cover my head in public. Refused to walk through the world as a messenger of Allah's teachings, ate hot dogs and bacon when I was with my girls. My Muslim beliefs lived just left of my heart. I was leaving space for something more promising. *Let her be who she's trying to become,* my father said. *Yeah,* I said. *Let me be myself.*

She was Sister Mama Loretta when our foreheads burned with fever, when our stomachs curled back over themselves and our heaving heads needed soft hands holding them. When we gathered over Monopoly boards and checker games we found ourselves laughing at her stories and begging her *Tell us another one, Sister Mama Loretta.* But she was not my mother. We all knew this.

At breakfast, when WWRL played Dorothy Moore singing "Misty Blue," my father fell silent over his food, his eyes furtive on the window, as though my mother would suddenly show herself, perched like a bird on the sill. *Oh, it's been such a long, long time. Look like I'd get you off of my mind.*

But my mother didn't show herself. I imagined her crazy, wild-haired and wide-eyed now, not the woman we knew before her ghost brother came back, the woman who ironed her blouses and spread her lips across her teeth to apply red lipstick.

═══

At night, I wrapped my head and kneeled alone, the apartment quiet with my brother and father at mosque where they prayed together, separate from the women. I pressed my forehead against the floor, my arms stretched out above me. We would be women, one day, Sylvia, Angela, Gigi, and I. There wouldn't be the world we were walking through, arm in arm, the ear against thigh on an afternoon of hair combing. There wouldn't be the cheek placed against beating hearts, the 10, 20, 30, 40, 50 song of a double Dutch game. When we were women, there would be nothing. We couldn't be friends, my mother had said. We couldn't trust us. And everywhere I looked, I saw glass shattering into truth.

=

When I was nine years old, Jerome looked up at my window and winked at me from where he and his friends were playing in the street. I didn't know how to wink back. I didn't know how to look down on his dark face and see promise there. The worlds of SweetGrove and Brooklyn hadn't yet merged into one world. So years later, when he grabbed my hand and said, *I know you*, I looked up at the teenager standing there and remembered so many things. *One day, you and me gonna do that thing*, he said. At twelve, I thought sixteen-year-old boys said this to every girl, so I nodded and said, *Okay.* He leaned down then, and kissed me.

Who could understand how terrifying and perfect it is to be kissed by a teenage boy? Only your girls, I thought.

Only your girls.

=

Sylvia was the baby of four sisters. Piano lessons. Dance lessons. On Sunday afternoons, when the family returned home from church, a French woman waited for the girls in the living room. *You must walk like this*, the woman said in French. *You must cross your legs like this when you sit. This is the salad fork, the dessert spoon, the glass for Bur-*

gundy. Angela, Gigi, and I watched from the door-way, stopped at entry by her mother's sharp eye. Beyond this point, the woman's brow said, you don't belong. Even here is too far. We heard the tone in the French words we did not understand. Crowded in that doorway, we were no longer lost and beautiful but ragged and ugly, made so by a flick of her mother's eye.

Still, Sylvia begged us to stay, begged her father with a girlish *Papá*, and then French words like a song falling from her mouth.

Photos of the four girls lined a room reserved just for sitting. There was a pool table in the basement, a refrigerator that dispensed ice. The two oldest sisters had already left for, as Sylvia's father called it, *University*. But Sylvia and her third sister each had a room painted the color of their choosing. Sylvia's room was pink. Her older sister's room was a pale gray. The older sister retreated to this room when we arrived, mysterious and evil. One Saturday she emerged from her room simply to slap Sylvia for laughing too loudly. Sylvia held her cheek silently. *It's against the rules to laugh like that*, she said finally. *I'm supposed to know we're better than that.*

But you always laugh that way, we said.

Not always, Sylvia said. *Not here.*

The parents questioned us. Who were our people? What did they do? How were our grades? What were our ambitions? Did we understand, her father wanted to know, the Negro problem in America? Did we understand it was up to us to rise above? His girls, he believed, would become doctors and lawyers. *It's up to parents*, he said, *to push, push, push.*

Once, as a young child, my mother asked me what I wanted to be when I grew up. *A grown-up*, I answered. She and my father laughed and laughed.

But listening to Sylvia's father, I felt myself straightening my back, tilting my chin up. Law, I wanted to say, like you. I want truth, I wanted to say. An absolute truth, or if not truth, reason—a reason for everything. But the hems of my bellbottoms were tattered. My socks in this shoeless house had holes in the heels. In the winter, because of my own absentmindedness, my hands and arms were often ashy. How could I even think of aspiring to anything when this was how I walked through the world? Sylvia's mother's flick of an eye said to us again and again, *Don't dream. Dreams are not for people who look like you.*

So I wanted to be Sylvia. And because I wanted it so much, I told her about my secret love, how Jerome and I met in my vestibule some evenings, his hands everywhere, his lips on my mouth, neck, breasts. How I had to stand on the upper stair to reach him. How he looked outside for grown-ups before leaving my building.

Sylvia's world felt delicate and foreign. Mother and father in one city, one home. Each room spare and clean. Beds were always made. Bookshelves dusted. Pots and pans put away into what her mother referred to as the pantry. Unstreaked mirrors hung above dressers. Bathrooms smelled of Pine-Sol.

There was fresh baked bread in a bread box. Peas and rice in Tupperware in the fridge. There were white knee-high socks folded in drawers, pantsuits hanging in closets, platform shoes neatly arranged on shoe racks. There was a painting of Haitian revolutionary Toussaint Louverture above the piano, another of Biafran leader Chukwuemeka Odumegwu Ojukwu between the velvet-curtained windows.

In the world of Sylvia's house, Angela, Gigi, and I sat with our feet crossed at the ankles, embarrassed suddenly by our bitten-down nails and frizzing hair. In this world, I wished for a head covering, a skirt that draped to the floor. We felt we had snuck into a party we had not been invited to. We feared breaking the china plates lined along the mantelpiece, speaking too loudly, laughing with our mouths open. Each side-eye glance from Sylvia's mother reminded us of how truly unworthy we were.

We saw the little girl Sylvia became there and tried to become little girls again, too.

Don't try to act like a dusty, dirty black American, Sylvia's sister said.

Sylvia's cheek reddened into her sister's handprint. It stayed that way for days and days.

Law. No one had this dream for me. No one held out a hand saying, *Here, take this.* So I told my secrets to Sylvia with the hope that I'd get something in return. I whispered how I fell in love slowly. First with the way Jerome called my name, *August,* so much breath around the sound that it was hard not to feel the summer light pouring out through his voice.

I was thirteen the first time we went further than the kisses we stole in the dark of my vestibule. Only Sylvia knew. Give this back to me, I wanted to say to her. I want your promised future filling up the empty space ahead of me.

10

But Gigi was the first to fly. A woman in white patent leather go-go boots came and got her from school one day so she could audition for a performing arts school in Manhattan.

Everybody, Gigi said. *Meet my mom.*

Hey, we said, struck silent by a woman so young and beautiful she could have been on the cover of *Ebony* or a centerfold in *Jet* magazine.

Hey yourselves, Gigi's mother said.

At the audition, Gigi told us she had to say the
same lines over and over—*Hey Big Daddy, ain't
you heard . . . the boogie-woogie rumble of a Dream
Deferred?*

Gigi said her lines again and again for us, her voice
deeper, strange, our Gigi but different, standing in
front of us inside someone else's skin.

*They said I had something. A white lady there said,
You could be someone.*

Then, suddenly, as though Sylvia's father looked
closely at us and saw every single thing he hated,
we were no longer Sylvia's friends but ghetto girls.
When we arrived late in the afternoon, he stood at
the door. *No company today*, he said to us. *Sylvia
needs to get ready for her new school.*

Go home, he said. *Study. Become somebody better
than you are.*

We could have blamed his stinging words on his stilted English. We could have said *Fuck you, man*—become who he thought we already were. But we were silent.

None of us asked, what new school. Or why. He was tall and thick, his hatred for us a deep wrinkle between his eyebrows.

We turned away from Sylvia's door, said good-bye to each other at the corner, each of us sinking into an embarrassed silence, ashamed of our skin, our hair, the way we said our own names. We saw what he saw when we looked at each other. So we looked away and headed home.

=

In class, Sylvia's empty seat reminded us of her father, his arms folded across his chest, his glare a reminder of a power that was becoming more and more familiar to us. A power we neither had nor understood.

When we saw Sylvia again a week later, she was wearing a St. Thomas Aquinas uniform, her older sister's arm tight around her shoulder. She glanced at us, mouthed, *Park later.* I squeezed Gigi's hand and nodded.

That evening, Sylvia pulled a joint from her coat pocket, let it slowly disappear into her mouth then pulled it out again, *To seal it,* she said. None of us asked where she'd gotten the joint or the Winston matchbook. We circled around her and watched her take the smoke deep into her lungs, hold it, then exhale. We followed her lead, the smoke hot and hard against the back of my throat. We had seen teenagers doing this, crowded together tight as fists, their eyes closed against the smoke. We coughed our way through, laughing at our own ig- norance until the laughter and the smoke seemed to release everything impossible in the world.

=

It was winter again and Angela had lost herself in dance, Gigi in lead role after lead role at the performing arts high school she now attended.

I spent my days watching people move, both outside our building and inside, too. Jennie was replaced by Carla, who stayed only a month before the police came and took her away. Carla was replaced by Trinity, a small, girlish man who spoke French to the men who followed behind him up the stairs in the evening.

At mosque the sisters asked, *What about their mother?* their eyes taking in my father's thin mustache, his thick close-cut head of hair, his broad shoulders. The manicured nails on his eight remaining fingers promised them damage, imperfection, and, they hoped, need.

Their mother is gone, my father answered.

Their mother's gone, Sister Loretta echoed.

What's in the urn, Daddy?

You know what's in that damn urn, August!

At night, I spoke to my mother, apologized for the lies my father told, promised her there'd come a day when he'd be less afraid. He'd take us back to Tennessee then, back to SweetGrove. I told her to be patient, that with Allah, all things were possible.

11

We turned thirteen and it seemed wherever we were, there were hands and tongues. There were sloe-eyes and licked lips wherever our new breasts and lengthening thighs moved.

Angela and Gigi and I showed up at Sylvia's house one Saturday morning when the family was gone. Sylvia, able to sneak us inside, stood ironing her Catholic school uniform as we talked. *It happened,* Angela said. *I'm bleeding.*

Finally, we said.

We thought you'd never join us on this side, we said.

We were teenagers now, our bodies different but all of us still the same height, all of us still blending into each other.

We found places to be together, sharing a joint on the stairs of the closed library, stepping over prayer rugs to sit on my bed, cutting two pizza slices into four at Royal Pizzeria because if we bought something, we could sit for hours. Park swings, handball courts, the spot of sun on the corner where a windowless factory set dozens of pale, tired women free every day at 5:00 P.M.

Angela said, *My mother said don't tell a soul.*

But we didn't have to open our mouths. Summer came again and men and boys were everywhere, feathery hands on our backsides in crowds, eyes falling too long at our chests, whispers into our

ears as we passed strangers. Promises—of things
they could do to us, with us, for us.

When Sylvia threatened to run away, her father
said we could stay over. He asked to call our parents, make sure they knew where we were. We
no longer looked at him—gave him our numbers
without lifting our eyes. Angela said, *My mother
already knows*, quickly before anyone could dial a
number, speak to someone. *It's fine*, Angela said,
looking anywhere else.

After speaking to my father, he said, *He's a good
man. He has his God. A man needs his God.* He
eyed Angela, the torn sweater, the hole in the toe
of her dingy socks. Angela tucked one foot behind
the other, bent into herself. Then, saying nothing,
he left.

We stayed up late, watching television sitcoms, eating Popsicles and bags of candy. Sylvia and I wore

baby-doll pajamas that felt obscene and made us giddy. We slow-danced with each other. Angela showed us how to French-kiss and we spent hours practicing. We practiced until our bodies felt as though they were exploding.

We whispered, *I love you* and meant it.

We said, *This is scary* and laughed.

When Jerome asked where I'd learned what I learned I said, *Don't worry about it* because he was eighteen and I was nearly fourteen and nothing mattered but hearing *I love you* and believing he meant it.

=

There were days when we sat in front of the television watching Clark Kent fall in love with Lois Lane and understood what it meant to hold secrets close. When Angela cried but wouldn't tell us why, we promised her our loyalty, reminded her

116

that she was beautiful, said *Knock, Knock, Angela. Let us in, let us in.* We stroked the sharp knots of her cheekbones, moved our fingers gently over her lips, lifted her shirt, and kissed her breasts. We said, *You're so beautiful.* We said, *Don't be afraid.* We said, *Don't cry.*

When she danced, her dance told stories none of us were old enough to hear, the deep arch of her back, the long neck impossibly turned, the hands begging air into her chest.

What are you saying, we begged. *Tell us what it is you need.*

But Angela was silent.

On the Fourth of July, my father took all of us to the East River, where thousands of people crowded to watch fireworks explode above the water. Pressed against each other, Angela whispered into my ear, *I'm gonna leave this place one day.*

I promised her we'd go with her.

But Angela shook her head, her straightened hair hot curled into a mushroom low over her brow and ears. She stared straight ahead at the fireworks.

Nah, she said. *Ya'll won't.*

That night, as New York and the rest of the country celebrated its independence, everywhere we looked, the world was red, white, and blue. We had shared a joint in the smoky bathroom of a crowded McDonald's and felt wild and giddy and free. On the subway home, someone's boom box played "50 Ways to Leave Your Lover" and we all laughed, singing along.

Hop on the bus, Gus. You don't need to discuss much.

Angela nodding, saying, *You know that's right!*

On a different planet, we could have been Lois Lane or Tarzan's Jane or Mary Tyler Moore or Marlo Thomas. We could have thrown our hats up, twirled and smiled. We could have made it after all. We watched the shows. We knew the songs. We sang along when Mary was big-eyed and awed by Minneapolis. We dreamed with Marlo of someday hitting the big time. We took off with the Flying Nun.

But we were young. And we were on earth, heading home to Brooklyn.

12

I looked for Jennie's children in the faces of strangers. The terrified girl with her hand closed tight around pieces of bologna, the boy with his too-small shoes. The night the woman came to take them, they had cried late into the day. My brother and I went down to get them, but the door was locked. *Open the door,* we said again and again. But even though we could hear them crying, they wouldn't open it. So we went back upstairs and turned the radio on.

They were on this side of the Biafran war, filling their mouths with whatever we offered, their stomachs never seeming full. Same dark skin. Same fearful eyes. Where had they been taken to this time?

Open the door, we said. *It's us. We have food upstairs. We can play hide-and-seek. Please open the door,* we said. *We can take you someplace better.*

We were not poor but we lived on the edge of poverty.

$$=$$

Alana moved in across the street. She wore men's suits and did the hustle with her green-eyed girlfriend inside the front gate, her perfect dome of an Afro bouncing. When she smiled, one side of her mouth went up followed by the other, and the four of us sat on the curb watching her, fascinated.

At night, when the DJs plugged extension cords into the streetlights, the four of us followed the line of brown and white cords to the music in the park. We watched neighborhood boys break-dance on flattened cardboard boxes and we screamed when the DJ threw Stevie Wonder's "Sir Duke" onto the turntable, and Jerome pulled me away from my girls. In the darkness, with Stevie singing, *They can feel it all over . . .* I let Jerome kneel down in front of me, pull my shorts to my knees, and put his mouth on me until my body, from neck to knees, exploded. I pressed my back into the cement wall of the handball court, trembling. The DJ had cut a slow song I didn't know into Sir Duke and I felt tearful suddenly. This was the temple I had promised Sister Loretta I'd protect, and now, cold suddenly, my shorts still down below my knees, I held Jerome's head a moment, his face soft and wet against my belly, then pushed him down again.

=

Temperatures broke the hundred-degree mark and we sweated through the days to get to nights in the park. Angela found a boy named John who had delicate fingers and spoke with a lisp. Sylvia's boyfriend was Jerome's age, pulling Sylvia away from us into the darkness behind the handball courts. Gigi said she was falling in love with Oswaldo, whose older brother had been killed in a gang fight with the Devil's Rebel's the summer before. We were afraid of the gangs and the fires that turned the wood-framed houses in our neighborhood to ash. But we had our guys and we had each other.

We knew the stories. Down on Knickerbocker a girl ran out of her house, her robe on fire. By the time she was safe, she was naked. On Halsey Street, a fireman carried two small children down the fire escape. For a long time, he couldn't pry their frightened arms from around his neck. I searched for the children's names in the paper, wondering if they had been Jennie's children.

At the end of the night, we pressed against our boyfriends, fingers locked together, slow swaying as the DJ announced, *We about to shut this party down, y'all.* Still, we held on to them, their skinny bodies as uncertain as our own of what we were moving toward. *Please,* they begged. And for a long time, we whispered back, *Not that. Not yet.*

—

Charlsetta had been sent away. She was sixteen, captain of the Thomas Jefferson cheerleaders. She had a straightened ponytail and bangs oiled and spiraling over her forehead. For weeks, we asked her younger brother where she'd gone. The whole block had heard the yelling. We had watched her mother leaving the house for work in the morning, stern-faced and stiff-backed. *Charlsetta got her behind beat last night,* we said to each other. *Her mother tore her up.*

And we laughed until the beating became legendary, a warning to all of us that this kind of public humiliation was only one belt-whipping away. There was some Charlsetta buried in each of us.

She got a baby inside her, her brother finally admitted. *She got sent back Down South.*

We pulled our boyfriends' fingers from inside of us, pushed them away, buttoned our blouses. We knew Down South. Everyone had one. Jamaica, Dominican Republic, Puerto Rico. The threat of a place we could end back up in to be raised by a crusted-over single auntie or strict grandmother.

Down South was full of teenagers like Charlsetta, their bellies out in front of them, cartwheeling in barren front yards as chickens pecked around them. We shivered thinking of Charlsetta's belly and imagined her and her boyfriend together while her mother was at work. How many times had they done it? How did it feel? When did she know?

We sat on stoops looking toward Charlsetta's house. We thought she'd come home with a pink-blanketed baby in her arms. We imagined her taking up her spot again on the squad, her blue and gold pom-poms in the air—*Come on team, fight-fight with all your might-might, get on the floor and let's score some more. Go boy!*—her ponytail bouncing, her bangs low over her eyes. When time passed and she didn't come home, we imagined she'd come home baby-less, the crusty auntie or pinch-faced grandmother raising the child as her own, sending Charlsetta back to her life in Brooklyn.

Autumn came and the DJs stopped setting up their amps and speakers in the park. The street-lights stopped flickering from the ebb and flow of stolen electricity. Our boyfriends begged, and again and again we said, *No.*

Charlsetta's brother broke both his arms at Bush-wick Park, the cast slings crisscrossing over his chest. *Is your sister back yet,* we asked him. Always, the answer was no. *Damn!* we said. *She's been gone forever.*

Was my father as absent as I remember? A folding chair in the kitchen and him in it, his head bent toward his hands, fingers moving over the bump where a thumb had once been, his black suit pants sharply creased by a too-hot iron so that there was a shine to parts of the fabric—a near-burntness that would remain, forever. Where had the fingers gone, my brother and I asked each other well into our teens. *A dog ate them,* we said. *His hands got stuck in a hole and he pulled and pulled until. Until.*

Winter came, and by late December Brooklyn was ankle deep in ice and snow. Platform shoes dominated New York, so we stumbled through the neighborhood in knee-high platform boots that zipped up the side but were anything but waterproof. I shivered through the winter, unsteady and half-frozen while my father stared down at his hands. He was living inside his faith by then, which left little room for understanding teenage girls. Where my brother and I had once been locked behind a half-open window, we were now more free than either of us could understand. Some evenings coming home I looked up to see my brother at the window, staring over the block, blank-eyed.

＝

A week after Christmas, a woman was found coatless and dead on the roof of the Marcy Houses projects. Women had been found dead before—in hallways, in basements, in the unlit corners of subway platforms. Sometimes, as we walked the streets, we imagined our own selves found somewhere. How long would it take to know? Who would be the first to ask, *Have you seen August? Have you seen . . . Angela . . . ?*

Angela said, *I don't know where my mother is.* Her voice was thick, a tremble to the words. I grabbed her hard, pulled her to me. *Angela,* I said, *she's fine.*

She's fine!

Sylvia and Gigi stood back, away from us so that
it felt like the world was spinning around an eye of
sorrow only Angela and I were inside of.

It's not her, Ang. I swear.

But it *was* her. A Medicaid card and a five-dollar
food stamp in her left coat pocket. A photo of Angela, front teeth missing, in her right. *Angela "An-
gel" Thompson, Age 7,* carefully written in ballpoint
pen. Someone at Kings County probably said *Lord,
I know that woman's child.*

Before we knew it was her mother, Angela spent
three nights at my house, the two of us curled together on the pullout sofa, my father in my bed.
Her hair smelled of sweat and Royal Crown hair
grease, her breath coming fast, even when she was
sound asleep. In the only light coming in from a
streetlamp, I stared at her and saw deep beneath

the smooth cheeks and broad nose, there she was—there was the woman staggering past us with her thin face, nearly toothless mouth, and Angela's eyes.

In the near darkness, I saw the roof, Angela's mother curled fetal against the cold. I saw the water. I saw Angela crumbling to the snow-covered ground. I saw my father kissing my mother goodbye, the satin lining her bed, the Bible against her chest, the thin gold band on her too-still finger. I opened my mouth to speak. Then closed it again. And stayed that way for a long, long time.

═

On the third morning, my father took the day off from work and took Angela to the police station. *This child's mama*, he said, *seems to be missing.*

We had never met Angela's mother. But now we knew we had seen her—in the clenching of fists as a pale woman staggered up our block, tried to hang on to a STOP sign and failed—as the dancing stopped and Angela bent toward us, away from her.

We had asked *What is it, Angela?* We said *Tell us.* We pressed our ears to her beating heart. . . .

She's not dead, Angela, I whispered. *They have the wrong person.*

When she pulled away from us days later, we didn't know to yank her back. We didn't say *Wait!* We said *We love you.* We said *See you tomorrow.* We said *Always and all ways, Ang.* We didn't say *Don't leave.* We didn't say *We'll come with you—wherever you go.*

We were teenagers. What did we know? About anything.

January came, and for days Sylvia disappeared into her Catholic school and pink room, safely tucked between her glaring mother and Merleau-Ponty–spouting father. Gigi stepped deep into the world of theater, rehearsing late into the evening, too tired, she said, to come around for a while.

She's not dead, Angela, I whispered again and again. *Don't believe them.*

But Angela wasn't me.

=

That's where I live, Angela had said one summer, pointing to a beautiful red-brick building some blocks away from us. But we had never been inside. Two weeks after the woman was found, Sylvia and Gigi returned to me, and together we pushed past the broken-lock foyer door and searched the mailboxes for Angela's last name. We didn't find it. *Does Angela live here?* we asked the people who came in and out of the building. *Nah,* they said. *I don't know no Angela.*

JACQUELINE WOODSON

When we called her number, a recording informed us that it had been disconnected. *Shit*, we said. *Damn!*

It wasn't her mother, I said to Sylvia and Gigi. *They made a mistake. Believe me. I know.*

We waited, shivering. Frayed and awkward now, the three of us too often falling silent.

My brother had grown tall and thoughtful. He loved Sister Loretta, followed the teachings of the Nation of Islam, and searched my face for anything he could find there.

You okay, August?

Yeah.

You sure.

134

Yeah.

What are you thinking about?

Nothing.

One evening, long after my father had gone to bed, but only days after Angela's mother had been found, he shook me awake.

=

You used to say she was coming back, he whispered. *Tomorrow and tomorrow and tomorrow.*

I pressed my eyes tighter together, turned toward the wall.

But you were wrong. She won't be coming back until the resurrection.

=

In Tennessee, honeysuckle vines bloomed thick and full in our yard every summer. My brother and I ran out in the early hours, barefooted and still in pajamas to suck the sweetness from the bright flowers. It was never enough. That faint hint of honeysuckle on the tongue an almost broken promise of something better hidden somewhere deeper.

You gonna make yourselves sick, our mother called from the screen door. Behind it, aproned and high-heeled, she was perfect, full-lipped and dark-skinned, her hair cut into an Afro. *Let that honeysuckle grow like you grow.*

The hair a halo. *Hallowed be thy name. On Earth as it is in Heaven.*

Her brother Clyde wasn't dead yet. He was sitting at our kitchen table smoking a Pall Mall and telling stories. We knew this only because he always smoked and we could hear our mother, ever so often laughing and saying, *Oh, you just telling stories, Clyde!* Saying, *And then what happened?* Saying, *I'm making catfish tonight. You staying for dinner?*

My brother and I ran through the fields, the high grass scratching our legs and feet, the sun beating down on us. This freedom was all we had ever known. Brooklyn was a place my father had come from. A hole closing up beneath him. We only knew SweetGrove and the words that ended every fairy tale our mother read to us. We lived in our own happily ever after.

=

But after her brother died, my mother began disappearing. First, there was the empty table at the end of the day, and me returning home from school to find my baby brother in the yard, searching for sugar snaps and berries, no beginnings of

meals in the house. My father arriving hours later
with bags of groceries—canned soups and pasta,
SpaghettiOs and frozen pizzas to be reheated on
the top of the wood-burning stove.

SweetGrove becoming memory. My mother becoming dust.

What's in the urn?

You know what's in the urn.

Is Mama home yet?

Memory like a bruise. Fading.

She's coming tomorrow and tomorrow and tomorrow.

Don't wade in the water, children.

Your mama's done troubled the water.

Our land moved in grassy waves toward the water. The land ended at the water. Maybe my mother had forgotten this.

And kept on walking.

13

We were not afraid of the dark places we went to with our boyfriends. Even though years before, a serial killer who called himself the Son of Sam had terrorized New York City, we backed into the darkened corners of the park anyway. Son of Sam killed white women. We were safe inside our brown skin.

But in Times Square that same year, brown girls were dying. Although we were miles away in Brooklyn, their stories felt close enough to touch, and haunted our nights. Those were the ones that were found, bodies rolled into rugs, behind trash bins, or naked and bobbing on the East River, throats slashed in the bathrooms of Forty-Second Street porn theaters. We knew that crossing that bridge meant being on the same side of the river as that place called Times Square, where girls like us got snatched up by pimps, shot up with dope, and spent the rest of their lives walking along Eighth Avenue, ducking their heads into slowing cars. This terrified us even more than losing Angela.

We'll see her on Monday, we said. But Monday never came. *She'll be back,* her teacher at Joe Wilson's School of Dance said. *Something has to come of that kind of talent.*

We were so afraid. Angela had been taken to a foster home on Long Island, we heard. Or was it Queens? With an aunt? Or was it a group home? We were fourteen. There was so much we didn't know.

=

One night, my father tiptoed in with another woman. I heard the ice clinking into glasses, heard the soft laughter. Rain beat down hard against the windows. The smell of damp surrounded us. I heard the soft plink of ice returning to the bottom of near-empty glasses. Where was Sister Loretta? I pulled my sheet over my head and reached for my brother's hand.

In the morning, the prayer rugs were still there but rolled up against the wall now. Outside, Brooklyn was bright blue. Cloudless. Already, kids screamed and called for each other on the street. When I tiptoed into the living room, the woman lying on his sofa bed pulled the covers up over herself but not before I saw the size of her breasts, the dark nipples.

You his baby girl? the woman asked.

=

Sylvia's father had a plan for her. One morning, Sylvia's first boyfriend showed up at her door. He was tall and brown-skinned, the captain of the neighborhood high school basketball team. *Please wait a moment*, her father said. When he came back, he pointed a .22 at her boyfriend's chest.

I will die in jail for my daughter, he said, his voice higher and softer than Sylvia had ever heard it. So high and soft, she couldn't scream. Just watched, her hand to her mouth, as her father lifted the gun higher and her boyfriend closed his eyes, begged, *Please God Please* until her father lowered his gun, said, *Go home to the God you believe in and don't ever come to my door again.*

He didn't know he had already lost Sylvia.

It hurt like hell, she whispered to us. *And then it didn't anymore. It didn't feel good like it's supposed to. But it didn't hurt.*

=

Please, Jerome begged. But I said, *No. Everything but that*, I said. At night I heard the woman who was not Sister Mama Loretta calling my father's name. In the morning, she pulled my father's robe together at her breasts, made instant coffee, and sat at our kitchen table, smoking.

Oh just do it, Sylvia said. *He's too fine to let slip away.*

=

Forget you then, Jerome said finally. *Forget you.*

Forget me.

=

I held on to my body and my brother held on to his faith, finally pulling my father back into it. On the weekends, they left the house in the early morning, spent the day at mosque, then returned late in the evenings, somber and soft-spoken, their Qur'ans tucked into the black briefcases they carried.

Other books began to fill our small bookshelf— *How to Eat to Live*; *Message to the Blackman in America*; *The Fall of America*. We sat together at the kitchen table late into the evenings, my father's and brother's heads deep inside their Nation of Islam books, me slowly turning the pages of my textbooks. I was suddenly hungry for the world outside of Brooklyn, something more complicated, bigger than this. Some evenings, my father looked over my shoulder, questioned me about geometry, *The Crucible*, the USSR. I stared at him, letting my shoulders rise and fall listlessly, the words too much trouble. My father patted my cheek, mumbled, *I have a woman I want you to meet*, and moved back to his Nation. I dipped my head back into my books. Because what else was there? Once, my brother and I

had sat at a window, watching the world. Now
we were deeply inside that world, working hard
to find our way through it. I cooked the foods
they would eat, omelets and eggplant, bean pies
and roasted vegetables, leafy salads topped with
tomatoes and onions, grilled fish, and olive oil. I
was nearly as tall as my father and our Saturdays
at Coney Island were long behind us. Hot dogs
and boiled corn from hawking vendors felt like
something out of another place and time.

The woman's office was small and smelled of musk
oil. Beneath her hijab, her face was unlined and
calm, so that at certain angles, she looked no older
than Jerome.

Brother, she said to my father.

Sister, he replied softly. *This is my daughter.*

There were degrees on the wall behind her, her
name in boldly inked letters.

August, she said, after my father left. *I want you to know you can trust me.*

August, she said. *Tell me about your mother.*

Orba (feminine), the Latin word for orphaned, parentless, childless, widowed. There was a time when I believed there was loss that could not be defined, that language had not caught up to death's enormity. But it has. *Orbus, orba, orbum, orbi, orbae, orborum, orbo, orbis . . .*

=

The shortcut from the subway meant walking through Irving Park, past the boys slamming balls into hoops and the handball players with their single-gloved hands. So many nights, this park transformed itself into a party, silhouettes of bodies moving to the DJ's music, couples disappearing into the deep pockets of it. But it was early spring and the DJs weren't jamming in the park yet. I walked through it slowly, my head down, my mind on the AP exam I'd be taking come Monday.

When I looked up, my eyes landed on Sylvia and Jerome, her head on his shoulder, her hands small and warm inside of his. I knew that warmth, that kind of holding.

Sylvia?

August. Hey.

Hey yourself.

When you're fifteen, pain skips over reason, aims right for marrow. I don't know how long I stood there staring at them, watching Jerome slip his hand from Sylvia's, watching Sylvia inch away.

Where're you heading?

When you're fifteen, the world collapses in a moment, different from when you're eight and you learn that your mother walked into water—and kept on walking.

When you're fifteen, you can't make promises of a return to the before place. Your aging eyes tell a different, truer story.

Linden, Palmetto, Evergreen, Decatur, Woodbine— this neighborhood began as a forest. And now the streets were named for the trees that once lived here.

It's crazy, Sylvia said. *The way this me-and-Jerome thing happened. Don't be mad. You guys broke up. I was gonna tell you.*

What about law? I wanted to ask. *What about your father?* The question vast as the silence between us: What about *me?*

My geography text had shown me the complexity of the world, and that night I leaned over it, hungrily, intrigued by all the places *out there* beyond Brooklyn—Mumbai, Kathmandu, Barcelona—anyplace but here.

In Fiji, so that the dead were not left alone in the next world, their loved ones were strangled in this one, the family reunited in the afterlife.

=

You said she was coming tomorrow and—my brother said.

For a long time, I believed it was true.

14

When did you first realize your mother had actually died? Sister Sonja wanted to know.

Outside, I could see the trees lining Fort Greene Park. It was clear out, warm, the beginning of spring. There was the rope of ivy on her window-sill, the leaves moving neatly along the ledge and down. There were gates on the windows, even though her office was only on the seventh floor. Had anyone ever vaulted past her? Jumped?

I looked up at her.

Why do you think my mother has died?

=

Three months passed before I saw Sylvia again. She was wearing her school uniform, her belly pushing against the buttons. She waved to me from across the street, two-way traffic between us.

August!

But I was leaving Brooklyn. I was already halfway gone.

=

It became the year of slipping into the pages of my textbooks and disappearing. It became the year of AP classes and PSAT review, of stretching toward something new, unfamiliar, a thing called the Ivy League. Because Bushwick had once been a forest and we had been called ghetto girls even though we were beautiful and our arms were locked together and our T-shirts blared our names and zodiac signs.

I pulled down the urn that had sat on the high bookshelf for as long as I could remember, lifted the top, and looked inside.

=

My mother walked into the water.

I moved the urn into the room I still shared with my brother, setting it on the nightstand beside my bed. All night long, I kept one hand pressed against it.

This earth is seventy percent water. Hard not to walk into it.

=

The night before Gigi landed the role of Mary Magdalene in the drama club's production of *Jesus Christ Superstar*, she called me, made me promise I'd be in the front row, beside Sylvia. *Let it go*, Gigi said. *The baby's already been made and you didn't want that boy anyway.* She said she'd put a coat on a seat in case Angela came back.

Can we do like olden times? Gigi said. *For me?*

But that night, as I pulled my coat on, I stopped, remembering Sylvia's belly and the urn filled with ashes and the boy who once winked up at me. I sat on the edge of my bed remembering running over the SweetGrove land and the sound of Clyde's laughter and my mother with a knife under her pillow and Sister Loretta's hands going in circles as she scrubbed the kitchen floor.

I sat there, the apartment silent, growing hot inside my coat. I sat there long after the play had ended.

Gigi faltered. During the last verse of "I Don't Know How to Love Him," a crack in her voice echoed through the auditorium. *Everyone laughed, I'd heard later. The whole auditorium. Everyone. We didn't mean to. We didn't know . . .*

Sylvia hadn't shown. Gigi's mother hadn't shown. The coats over the seats Gigi had saved for us remained there until her castmates took theirs and only hers remained.

Two steps to the left or right or back or front and you're standing outside your life.

Someone's friend knew someone who lived at the Chelsea Hotel. The cast party was on the eleventh floor.

Who was there to see Gigi lift her heels up and fly?

That year, her hair had grown long past her back. Most days she pulled it up into a braid. But on the evening of the performance, she'd worn it out, letting it fan over her shoulders. Did it lift like a dark wing into the Chelsea night? Did she really believe there was nothing on the other side of fifteen?

If the tribes of the Fijis send their living off to join their dead, it should have been me flying. Or Angela. But we remained on earth. Believing ourselves wingless.

15

When I stepped off the bus in Providence, Rhode Island, I was alone. I had wanted this—to step outside of Brooklyn on my own, no past, just the now and the future.

Auggie, I corrected the professor on my first day. *My name is Auggie. I'm here because even when I was a kid, I wanted a deeper understanding of death and dying.*

That's crazy, the white devil of a boy who would become my first lover turned to me and said, his skin so pale I could see the blue veins running through it. *Me, too.*

How do you begin to tell your own story? The first time I heard the Art Ensemble of Chicago, I called out Gigi's name. How could any of us have known? Roscoe Mitchell on saxophone, Lester Bowie on trumpet, the stumbling together of horns and drums and bells into music until so much beauty rose into the world breathing had to be remembered again, forced. How had Sylvia's philosophy-spouting father missed this? How had my own father, so deep inside his grief, not known there were men who had lived this, who knew how to tell his story? How had the four of us, singing along to Rod Stewart and Tavares and the Hues Corporation, not turned our radio just that much to the right or left and found Cecil Taylor, Ornette Coleman, Miles Davis?

And when we pressed our heads to each other's hearts how did we not hear Carmen McRae singing? In Angela's fisted hands, Billie Holiday staggered past us and we didn't know her name. Nina Simone told us how beautiful we were and we didn't hear her voice.

I spent my twenties sleeping with white boys in photo-less rooms filled with jazz. As I pushed their resistant heads down, I thought of Brooklyn, of Jerome and Sylvia and Angela and Gigi. I cried out to the sounds of brown boys cursing and Bowie's trumpet wailing. When I pulled my lovers into me, my eyes closed tight against the faces I had grown up believing belonged to the devil, I imagined myself home again, my girls around me, the four of us laughing. All of us alive.

In the Philippines, a beautiful brown man pressed his lips to my feet again and again, saying, *Always begin here.* In Wisconsin, I promised my housemate turned lover that I'd stay with her always. Months later, as the scattered pages of my dissertation lay finished and approved on the floor beneath us, I kissed her slightly parted lips as she slept and left in the night. In Bali, I waited at night for a beautiful black man from Detroit to show up in the dark. *Say it*, he begged, our bodies moving against each other with such a hunger, we laughed out loud. *It's just three damn words.*

I turned thirty in Korea, cried for a week because I thought I was pregnant. Then cried for another when it was certain I was not. In the background, Abbey Lincoln sang "It's Magic" and I saw again the view of our block from a high-up window, the children playing below my brother and me.

Once in a café in San Francisco the woman I had lived with for eight months asked why did I sleep with fisted hands.

Do I?

Yeah, you do, she said.

Once I came very close to saying *For a long time, my mother wasn't dead yet.* But didn't.

16

In the autumn of my sixteenth year, my father took us back to SweetGrove. We rode the train to Tennessee then rented a car and drove an hour to where our land had once been. The leaves were beginning to turn, but the air was still thick with heat. We arrived in the early evening. My brother and I slammed out of the car like we were children again, running down the long dirt road that lead to the house. But where our house had once been, there were weeds now, taller than any of us and thick as poles. From where we had stopped, I could smell the briny water. We stood there, silent. In the silence, we could hear the soft lap of the lake.

I took my brother's hand and together, silently, we walked toward it. Orange signs were nailed to the trees around us. NO TRESPASSING. PRIVATE LAND. DO NOT CROSS. But we kept on walking. The water was dark, near black against the brightly colored trees.

When did you realize your mother was actually dead, Sister Sonja would ask again months later.

Never. Every day. Yesterday. Right at this moment.

When my father took us back to the water.

I could hear our father approaching. Even here, so far away from Brooklyn, his soft, slow steps were as familiar as time.

Way out, I could see a person in a canoe, gently paddling along the line of pine trees. At its deep-est point, the water dropped down to twenty feet. *I've only ever put my toes in,* my mother would say.

166

*I just needed to feel it against my feet, that's all. And
be close by.*

=

At the diner, after my father's funeral, my brother
suddenly asked, *Why did you always say that? Why
did you always tell me she was coming tomorrow and
tomorrow and tomorrow?*

For a long time, I said nothing, then finally, *Because I believed it was true. That one of these tomor-
rows, she'd get here.*

Someplace off the coast of South Carolina, a tribe
of Ibo people brought over by slave catchers tossed
themselves into the water. They believed that since
the water had brought them here, the water would
take them home. They believed going home to the
water was far better than living their lives enslaved.

=

When I see Angela again, I am in my first year at Brown, sitting in my room on a Friday night. A boy I am planning to sleep with has his head on my lap. She appears suddenly on the television screen, darker than I remember her, her hair long and straightened. But her face is the same, angled and beautiful. The movie is about a dancer hungry for the lead role in *La Sylphide*, as her fiancé runs off and her own real life mirrors the story. Angela is stunning as she dances across the stage, her body thinner than I remember, but muscled and able. When she dances toward the camera, I call out to her.

Angela!

The boy asks if I know her.

She's hot, he says.

Angela, I whisper. *You made it.*

=

Behind my brother and me, my father was saying that it was time to move on now, but none of us moved from where we were standing.

Wind came up, shuddering the leaves. The person in the canoe had stopped paddling and now cast a line into the water. Perch. Trout. Maybe catfish but I'm not sure.

This is memory.

I watched the water slowly lap back and forth against the shore. The sun was beginning to set. I took my brother's hand and held it. We had no people left in Tennessee. We'd stay the night in a hotel, buy some souvenirs somewhere. In the late afternoon tomorrow, we'd get back into our rented car and begin the long journey home to Brooklyn.

I lifted my head to look up into the changing leaves, thinking how at some point, we were all headed home. At some point, all of this, everything and everyone, became memory.

ON WRITING
ANOTHER BROOKLYN

Creating a novel means moving into the past, the hoped for, the imagined. It is an emotional journey, fraught at times with characters who don't always do or say what a writer wishes. I am often asked to explain this and find that I can't—when I am inside my novel, it makes sense. But once I emerge from the world I've created, I find it difficult to go back to the moments before my characters walked through it with me. I guess in many ways, the characters a writer creates have always existed *somewhere*.

Long before I began to sketch the lives of August, Gigi, Angela, and Sylvia, I was thinking about what it means to grow up girl in this country—remembering and imagining, as the poet Rilke wrote, "the powerful, the uncommon, the awakening of stones." So while *Another Brooklyn* is a work of fiction, for the years the story took to feel "done," I have lived inside the lives of my characters, asking questions of myself about their own survival—who makes it big, who doesn't, who lives, what will they wear, do, say, how long or short is their hair, how old will they be at the beginning, in the end?

Who will they love? How will they leave us, and what will they leave behind?

And, most of all: What is the bigger story?

I do know that as the novel takes shape on the page, it's hard for characters' lives not to intersect with the writer's own life. As we unpack our characters' stories and actions, it's hard not to unpack our own history. In *Another Brooklyn,* I looked back to my teenage years, mining them, rediscovering the deep love I had for my friends, the startling joy and fear of first loves, the will's intensity to survive, and the slow-motion ferocity of the end of childhood.

When I started writing *Another Brooklyn*, I wanted to write about the bonds we share as young people and of all the parables of those bonds. I wanted to set this story in Bushwick—the neighborhood of my childhood, the neighborhood I once knew so well.

A writer writes to hold on. I wanted the Bushwick of my childhood remembered on the page—so I created four girls who were fascinating and foreign to me, stepping far outside of my own childhood. Then I sat them down in a neighborhood that was once as familiar to me as air.

I did not know what August, Sylvia, Angela, and Gigi would do or how they would do it. I did not know who would live and who wouldn't. I did not yet know how I would feel, or how I wanted to feel, in the end. But I wrote toward the hope and longing for the girls' survival. I wrote toward the questions I had as though I could plow through them with my own words and emerge more conscious and clearheaded.

Do I know more now? About girlhood? About what it means to be a woman of color, vibrant and visible and adored? About what it means to hold on to that love and then, just as quickly, let it go? I think so . . .

Another Brooklyn took me on a journey. I looked up from the finished manuscript a little older, more thoughtful, and ever thankful for the village of women who have supported me as I wrote: my partner, Juliet Widoff; my sisters from other mothers—Linda Villarosa, Jana Welch, Toshi Reagon, Bob Alotta, An Na, Cher Willems, Nancy Paulsen, Kathleen Nishimoto, Kirby Kim, Charlotte Sheedy, Jane Sasseen, Jayme Lynes, Odella Woodson . . . this list could go on and on.

My brothers from other fathers—Ellery Washington, Nick Flynn, Chris Myers, Kwame Alexander, Jason Reynolds . . . this list, too, could go on and on.

This book wouldn't be here without my crew from the past—Donald Douglas, Michael Mewborn, Maria and Sam Ocasio, Renée and Emilio Harris, Sophia Ferguson, and Pat Haith.

Tracy Sherrod and Rosemarie Robotham

both helped me to shape this novel into something people living outside my head could understand. Thank you.

At the day's end, a writer lives alone with her story, wrestling with characters and settings, and the way light filters into and out of a scene. The deeper messages often escape her. Sometimes I take for granted the journey through the telling. At other times I curse the muse's power. But through it all, I live each day in deep gratitude.

—JW